B H. Ravey

The
Wishing Wand
and
Other Stories

by
ENID BLYTON

Illustrated by

Martine Blaney

AWARD PUBLICATIONS

For further information on Enid Blyton please contact
www.blyton.com

ISBN 1-84135-446-5

Text copyright 1946 Enid Blyton Limited
Illustrations copyright © 1993 Award Publications Limited

Enid Blyton's signature is a trademark of Enid Blyton Limited

First published by Sampson Low as *Enid Blyton's Holiday
Book Series*

This edition entitled *The Wishing Wand and Other Stories*
published by permission of Enid Blyton Limited

First published by Award Publications Limited 1993
This edition first published 2005

Published by Award Publications Limited, The Old Riding
School, Welbeck Estate, Nr Worksop, Notts S80 3LR

Printed in Singapore

CONTENTS

The Wishing Wand

Once there was great excitement in Feefo Village because the Lord Chamberlain had promised wishing wands to all the pixies and fairies.

"You have behaved very well this year," said the Chamberlain. "Every one has been kind and good, so, on the first day of spring, I will come to each house and give all of you a wishing wand."

Now pixies and fairies long to have a wishing wand more than anything else in the world, because if they have a magic wand their wishes will come true. So you can imagine that everyone in Feefo Village was very excited.

Most excited of all were the two

pixies who lived in Corner Cottage. They hadn't always been very good, but that year they really had tried their best – and now they were to have a wishing wand like everyone else. They *were* pleased!

When the day came for the wands to be given to each of them, the two pixies, Pickle and Goof, went out into their little front garden to enjoy the sunshine of the first day of spring. They had on their best suits, for they knew that the Lord Chamberlain would call on them before long.

They sat on the edge of their well and waited. They talked about their wands.

"I shall wish such a lot of wishes with my wand," said Pickle. "I shall wish for a pair of new shoes, to begin with. I haven't had a new pair for years, and my old ones look dreadful with this nice new suit."

"I shall wish for a new hat, with a pink feather," said Goof.

"A *pink* feather!" said Pickle, "Why a

pink feather? Pink's an ugly colour."

"It isn't," said Goof. "It's lovely. Why, roses are pink, aren't they, and the sunset clouds? So I shall have a pink feather. And what's more, I shall wish for pink cushions on the kitchen chairs, and a pink carpet on the floor."

"Indeed you won't," said Pickle. "I won't have pink things all over my kitchen. I shall wish for blue."

"And I shall wish for a nice, large, brown dog," said Goof, taking no notice of Pickle. "One that will belong to me and nobody else."

"You can't wish for a dog," said Pickle at once. "You know how we've always said we'd have a cat. Well, I want a cat, and your dog won't get on with it. I shall wish for a cat with long, long claws that will scratch your dog if you wish for one."

"Be quiet, Pickle," said Goof crossly. "I'm thinking of my wishes. My dog will eat your cat if you are so silly as to wish for one. I shall wish for a motor-car too – a yellow one with blue spots."

"How terrible!" said Pickle. "I won't be seen out in a car like that."

"Well, you needn't come out with me if you don't want to," said Goof. "I can go out with Gobo or Tinks."

"Whatever car we have I shall share," said Pickle crossly. "And I tell you I won't have a yellow one with blue spots. I shall wish for my own car – it shall be dark blue with red wheels."

"Our garage will only take one car," said Goof. "So you'll have to put up with mine. Ha ha!"

Pickle glared at him. "Then I shall wish for another garage!" he said. "And I shall put my car in that."

"You can't wish for another garage," said Goof. "There are houses each side of us, and there's no room for one. Ha ha, again!"

"Stop ha-ha-ing at me!" said Pickle, getting really angry. "If I want another garage I shall have one. I shall wish away the houses next door, and then there will be plenty of room for a garage for my blue car."

"You wicked pixie!" cried Goof. "How dare you wish away Dame Clap's house and Mr Tibs' house! What would they do?"

9

"Oh, I'd wish away their houses to the hilltop over there," said Pickle. "And if you aren't careful I might wish you and your horrid dog away to the hilltop too."

"*Pickle!*" cried Goof in horror. "You wouldn't do such a thing!"

"Well, *I* don't want to live with a person who wears pink feathers and drives about in a yellow motor-car with blue spots. So there!"

"Pickle, if you aren't very careful, I shall wish you a hard smack," said Goof solemnly. "Yes, a very hard smack that you won't like at all."

"And who'll smack me I'd like to know?" shouted Pickle angrily. "Not you, Goof, I know that!"

"Oh yes I would," said Goof. "I can hit hard."

"You can't," said Pickle. "I wouldn't let you. I'd slap you first!"

"Oh no, you wouldn't," said Goof.

"Oh yes, I would," said Pickle.

"Oh no, you wouldn't," said Goof. "I'd get my slap in first – like that!"

And he slapped Pickle hard on the arm. Pickle gave a roar of rage and smacked Goof on the chest. Goof slapped Pickle on the cheek and Pickle hit Goof so hard on the nose that poor Goof fell backwards, lost his balance – and disappeared down the well!

"Oooooh!" shrieked Pickle in fright, for he hadn't meant to push Goof down the well. He clutched at him and caught Goof's leg – but alas for Pickle! he fell over the edge too, and down

they both went – down, down, down, into the dark, cold water at the bottom.

Splash! They hit the water, went under and bobbed up again. The well was not very deep. They could just stand – but, oh dear, how in the world were they to get out again! The sides of the well were made of brick and were steep and smooth. It was no use trying to climb out.

"Let's shout!" said Goof, shivering. So they shouted, "Help! Help! We're down the well!"

But their voices were lost in the deep

round well, and nobody heard.

It was a pity they had fallen down the well just at that moment, because the Lord Chamberlain came down the lane to their house, to give them their wishing wands. He went up the path to the front door and knocked. Nobody answered, of course, because the two pixies were at the bottom of the well. The Lord Chamberlain knocked again and again. Still no answer.

"Most extraordinary," said the Chamberlain crossly. "Nobody about at all, and orders were given to everyone who wanted a wand to be at home today. Well, if Pickle and Goof are not at home they can't have their wands. I shall send them back to the Fairy Queen, and she can give them to someone else."

He went to the next house. He didn't hear Goof and Pickle calling and shouting. Nobody heard them at all, and it wasn't until Mother Clap came to get some water that evening, that the pixies were found.

"Ooooooh!" shrieked Mother Clap, when she saw two round, white faces looking up at her from the bottom of the well. "What's down there – what's down there?"

"It's only us," shouted Goof. "It's Goof and Pickle. We fell down. Get a ladder for us, dear Dame Clap."

"I can do something better than that for you," said Dame Clap, and she took her wishing wand and waved it over the well. "I wish you both out here beside me."

At once Pickle and Goof flew out of the well and landed in surprise beside Dame Clap.

"Oh dear! Has everyone got their wands?" said Goof sadly.

"Everyone but you," said Dame Clap. "The Chamberlain said you weren't at home this afternoon, so he has sent your wands back to the Queen. Whatever were you doing?"

"Well-er-well, we-we just fell down the well," said Goof, feeling very much ashamed. "That's all."

"Quarrelling again, I suppose!" said Dame Clap. "I thought you had given that up, and meant to behave yourselves. Well, you've lost your wishing wands *this* year – and serve you right, if you can't be nice to one another!"

Off she went, and left Goof and Pickle alone. They looked at one another, very red in the face.

"Sorry, Goof," said Pickle in a small voice.

"Sorry, Pickle," said Goof in a smaller voice. Then, arm in arm, they went indoors to get dry. Weren't they a couple of sillies?

Mr Big-Hat's Button

"Dame Pippy, I want you to turn out my big cupboard," said Mr Big Hat, the wizard.

"Yes, Mr Big-Hat," said Dame Pippy. She came in to work for the wizard every day. She was a little bit afraid of him because he knew such powerful magic. When he was making spells she always locked herself away in the kitchen.

"You never know when he's going to use thunder and lightning in his spells, or a dozen black cats," she said to her friends. "And my! What a temper he's got! I never dare to peep into any of his books, or even so much as open his desk!"

"I should think not, Dame Pippy!"

16

said Mother Woolly, her friend. "That wouldn't be very honest. It never does to peep and pry, or to take even the smallest thing that belongs to anyone else!"

"As if I would!" said Dame Pippy crossly. "My word, I'm scared even to dust, with all the magic about that place!"

When she turned out Mr Big-Hat's cupboard Dame Pippy found a lot of interesting things. There were big, old books of forgotten spells. There were bottles of strange-smelling liquids that changed colour as she looked at them. There were boxes of strange powders that made her sneeze if she opened them.

"My word! There must be a lot of old magic about this cupboard!" thought Dame Pippy. "And isn't it dusty! Now, what's in this tin that rattles so?"

She cautiously opened the tin. Inside was a collection of buttons. You should have seen them!

There were all sizes and shapes and colours – red and blue and green and yellow, round and square and oblong, big and small.

"The pretty things!" said Dame Pippy, and she ran her fingers through them. "I'd like to have these buttons in my work-basket! That's where they ought to be, not in this dusty old cupboard, where no one will ever see them or use them."

But she didn't dare to take the tin of buttons and put it into her work-basket. Dear me! Mr Big-Hat might fly into one of his dreadful tempers if she did such a thing as that!

She was just shutting down the lid when she saw a very bright red button, perfectly round, with five little holes in

the middle of it. She looked at it.

"Now I do believe that would match the missing button on my husband's red dressing-gown," she thought. "Yes, I do believe it would!"

She took it out and put it back again. Then she took it out again. "Mr Big-Hat would never miss a little red button like that," she thought to herself. "Why, I don't suppose he even knows there's a whole *tin* of buttons here. It would be silly of me not to take this little button, now I've seen it. I'm sure it would match perfectly, and it's just the right size."

19

Without thinking any more about it, Dame Pippy took the round red button from the tin and slipped it into her apron pocket. Then she shut the tin, put it back on the shelf and went on cleaning out the cupboard.

When she got home that night she took out her husband's dressing-gown and put the little red button against the other buttons. But, alas, it didn't match at all! It wasn't a bit the same colour. Bother!

She put it on the table and left it there. Soon Mother Woolly came in for a chat and she saw the button there.

"My! Do you want that?" she said. "I believe it would just match the buttons on the jersey of the little boy next door. He's lost one."

"Well, take it," said Dame Pippy, though she knew quite well she had no right to say that at all! It wasn't hers to give – and it hadn't been hers to take, either!

Mother Woolly stayed for a while and then went home, taking the button with her. Dame Pippy forgot all about it until the next day. Then she got a horrid shock.

"When you turned out that cupboard of mine, did you happen to see a tin of buttons?" asked Mr Big-Hat.

Dame Pippy went red. "Y-y-yes, sir," she said.

"Good!" said Mr Big-Hat. "I hoped they would be there. Get the tin for me, Dame Pippy. I want a special button out of it."

Dame Pippy went to get the tin. Oh, my goodness! How she hoped it

wouldn't be that silly little red button that Mr Big-Hat wanted!

He took the tin from her and emptied all the buttons on to his table. "It's a scarlet button," he said. "Quite round. With five little holes in the middle. A very, very special button, for use in a very powerful spell. It's a button off the dress of one of the cleverest witches that ever lived. Must be chock-full of magic. Now, where is it?"

Dame Pippy couldn't say a word. Her knees shook. That button! She knew it wasn't there. She had given it to Mother Woolly. Oh why, why had she been so foolish as to take it?

"Strange!" said Mr Big-Hat in a cross voice. "It doesn't seem to be here. Dame Pippy, it must have rolled out into the cupboard. Will you please

go and look – and go *on* looking in that cupboard till you find it. It is *most important.*"

"Y-y-y-y-yes, sir," stammered poor Dame Pippy.

She went off to the room where the cupboard stood. What was the use of looking? She knew the button wasn't there. But she dared not tell the wizard. No, no, she'd rather run away and never come back!

She heard him putting his big iron pot on his fire to boil. Ah, that meant he was beginning to make a spell. He would be busy for quite a while. She would have time to rush out to Mother Woolly's and get back that button!

Dame Pippy slipped out of the back door, still trembling. She saw that the smoke from Mr Big-Hat's chimney had suddenly turned yellow. That meant he was making a very powerful spell indeed – a spell that might want that button! She must be quick!

She banged on Mother Woolly's door. "Did you give that red button to the little boy next door?" she cried. "I want it back!"

"Yes, I gave it to his mother," said Mother Woolly. "Why?"

But Dame Pippy did not wait to answer. She ran next door and banged on the door there. "Funny!" thought Mother Woolly. "She's come out without her coat or hat and in her old working slippers. And it's raining!"

"Could I have that red button Mother Woolly gave you?" begged Dame Pippy when the woman of the house came to the door. "Did you put it on your boy's jersey?"

"No. It didn't match," said the woman. "I gave it to John to play with. Johnny, what did you do with that button?"

"I gave it to my cousin Ella," said John. "She said she had lost one of her red tiddly-winks, so I thought the button would do instead. She lives up the hill, Dame Pippy."

"Oh dear!" said Dame Pippy, and tore up the hill in the rain, her hair getting wetter and wetter. She came to the house of Johnny's cousin Ella and banged on the door.

"*Have* you got that red button that John gave Ella?" she asked. "I need it back. It's most important."

"Oh, Ella was playing tiddly-winks with it, when Too-Tall came in," said Ella's mother. "And he said he would like to have the button to sew on a red belt he has – it was just the right size. I gave it to him."

"Oh, *my!*" said poor Dame Pippy. "Mr Too-Tall lives miles away – and it's pouring with rain. Why didn't I bring an umbrella!"

Off she went again, her shoes quite soaked through, her breath coming in pants and puffs. Mr Too-Tall lived in the woods. Dame Pippy got there at last and asked Mr Too-Tall please, please to give her back the red button.

"Well, I sewed it on a red belt I had and gave it to my sister Katie," said Too-Tall. "I've no doubt she will give it to you if you ask her. How wet you are! Wait a minute and I'll lend you an umbrella."

But Dame Pippy couldn't wait. She rushed off again to Mr Too-Tall's sister Katie.

But she had gone to a working-meeting, so Dame Pippy had to toil all the way across the fields to Mrs Busy's house, where the working-meeting was being held.

"Bless us all! How wet you are!" said Dame Busy. "And look at your shoes! Come in and tell me what you want."

Dame Pippy panted out what she had come for. She looked for the belt on Katie's waist. But it wasn't there.

"I'm so sorry – but the red button came off the belt whilst I was walking here," said Katie. "Too-Tall didn't sew it on properly. So off came the button and down dropped my belt. I picked up the belt – but I couldn't find the button. It dropped somewhere by the stile."

Almost crying now with the wet and the cold, poor Dame Pippy stumbled off to the stile to look for the dropped button. And after she had gone down on her hands and knees and crawled about in nettles and grass and other weeds for half an hour, she actually found the scarlet button.

Tears of relief ran down her cheeks. She had got it at last. She ran all the way back to Mr Big-Hat's, hoping that he hadn't yet finished his spell.

But he had. The chimney smoke was no longer yellow. Mr Big-Hat was standing with his finger on the bell in his work-room, ringing and ringing for Dame Pippy. Why didn't she come? It was long past his dinner time. He was hungry.

Where was Dame Pippy?

"R-r-r-r-r-r-ring!" went the bell, as Dame Pippy staggered in through the back door. She ran straight to Mr Big-Hat's work-room, panting, her hair dripping wet and her clothes soaking.

"Oh, sir! I've been looking for that

button!" she said. "And I've got it!"

She held out her hand with the scarlet button lying in the palm. But Mr Big-Hat didn't take it.

"I made a mistake," he said. "It wasn't that red button I needed after all. It was a blue one. I don't want that red one. There's no magic in it."

Well! After all she'd done, to think it was the wrong button! Dame Pippy threw her wet apron over her head and sobbed loudly. Mr Big-Hat was astonished. He saw how wet Dame Pippy was. What *had* she been doing?

"I've been all over the place for that red button," sobbed Dame Pippy. "And now you don't want it."

"But why did you go all over the place?" asked Mr Big-Hat, even more astonished. "It was in the cupboard, surely?"

"It wasn't. I wanted a red button to match one missing from my husband's dressing-gown," sobbed Dame Pippy. "And I took *your* red button. It *would* be the one you asked for! And then you

didn't want it after all. A-tish-oo! A-tish-oo!"

"You have caught a dreadful cold," said Mr Big-Hat. "Oh, Dame Pippy, it would have been so much better to have confessed that you had taken the button when I asked you for it this morning!"

"It would have been better not to have taken it at all!" said Dame Pippy, tears pouring down her cheeks. "Now you'll tell me to go. Now I shan't be able to work for you any more. Nobody will let me work for them. I shall lose all my friends. How dreadful for such big things to happen to me because of one tiny red button!"

"Yes, Dame Pippy – it's surprising how often big sorrows come out of small sins," said Mr Big-Hat sadly. "But cheer up – this time the big things are not going to happen. You have punished yourself enough, without my punishing you, too. Go and get some dry things on – and some dinner for us – and I'll make a fine big spell to stop you having a very bad cold!"

Well, dear me, Dame Pippy suddenly felt much better after that. She rushed out to get some dinner for poor, hungry Mr Big-Hat. She'd been silly and wrong and not very honest – but she'd be better now. She'd never so much as take a pin. Then Mr Big-Hat made her a spell to cure a bad cold – and he put into it the red button, which turned out to have some quite good magic in it. So, as Mr Big-Hat said, it was a good thing Dame Pippy found it after all!

Mr Stamp-About's Walking Stick

"Where's my walking stick gone?" shouted Mr Stamp-About, coming into the kitchen in a great rage. "It's gone *again*. It's not in the hall-stand where it should be. What have you done with it? What have you done with it?"

Mrs Stamp-About blinked at her angry husband. "Don't shout so, dear," she said. "Didn't you lend your stick to Mr Flap the day before yesterday?"

"Well, if I did, why hasn't he brought it back?" yelled Mr Stamp-About. "Why isn't it in the hall-stand?"

"Oh, go and ask him, dear," said his wife. So off went Mr Stamp-About, stalking down the street to Mr Flap's house. He banged at the door.

"Oh, it's you, Stamp-About," said

Mr Flap. "Don't break my knocker, *please*! What do you want?"

"My stick that I lent you," said Stamp-About.

"Oh, your stick. Well, I gave it to old Dame Shuffle yesterday," said Mr Flap. "She was limping badly. She said she would leave it at your house."

"Well, she didn't. It isn't in the hall-stand," said Mr Stamp-About, his face getting red again. "It never *is* in the hall-stand. Why isn't it there?"

"Go and ask Dame Shuffle," said Mr Flap, getting tired of Stamp-About, and he shut his door. Mr Stamp-About stamped off down the road, round the corner, and up the hill to Dame

Shuffle's cottage. She was in her garden. Mr Stamp-About shouted to her.

"Where's my stick that Mr Flap lent you and told you to bring back to me? It's not in my hall-stand."

"Oh, your stick? Well I found I couldn't walk all the way to your house with it after all," said Dame Shuffle, "so I gave it to Father Frown, and he said he'd drop it in for you when he passed by your house."

"Well, he didn't. And it isn't in my hall-stand," said Mr Stamp-About. "I'd like to know why!"

"Go and ask Father Frown," said Dame Shuffle, "and don't shout so. It

goes right through my head."

She went indoors. Mr Stamp-About went off, fuming, to find Father Frown. He lived at the other end of the village. He was leaning on his front gate, smoking a pipe.

"Hey, Father Frown!" yelled Mr Stamp-About, almost deafening him. "Where's my stick? It's not in my hall-stand, and that's where it should be. Dame Shuffle gave it to you to drop in at my house when you passed by."

"So she did," said Father Frown. "But I found I wasn't going your way after all, so I asked the butcher if he would mind giving it to you when he brought the meat today."

"Well, he didn't bring it and I'd like to know why," said Mr Stamp-About, beginning to rage again.

"You'll burst one day if you go on like this," said Father Frown, frowning hard. "If you want to know why he didn't bring your stick, go and ask him. He lives in the village. It's on your way home."

Stamp-About stalked down the village to Mr Joint, the butcher. Mr Joint was cutting up some meat. He didn't like Mr Stamp-About at all.

"Where's that stick of mine?" said Mr Stamp-About.

"How should *I* know?" said the butcher. "In your hall-stand, I expect."

"Then you expect wrong," shouted Stamp-About. "It's not. Father Frown gave it to you to deliver with the meat, and you didn't. Why not?"

"Because I didn't deliver any meat to you today," said Mr Joint. "You had fish from the fish-shop as you very well know. As for your stick, I gave it to your friend Mr Hallo, when he came for sausages this morning. He said he would take it to you at once."

Mr Stamp-About went out of the

36

shop. He was thinking hard. Yes, Hallo had come to see him. Had he given him back his stick? He couldn't remember it. Surely it would be in the hall-stand if he had? No, no, Hallo hadn't given him his stick. He had kept it himself.

He went off to Mr Hallo's house. Hallo lived next door but one to Stamp-About. He was in his garden, weeding.

"Hallo, Hallo!" said Mr Stamp-About, in rather a cross voice. "Why didn't you give me my stick this morning when you came to see me?"

"I did," said Hallo, at once. "But you were so excited because you'd noticed a whole lot of ripe plums on your plum tree that you hardly thanked me."

"Well, my stick isn't in my hall-stand," said Mr Stamp-About. "Where is it?"

"How should I know?" said Hallo, crossly. "You are always in such an excitement about something or other that I wonder you ever remember where anything is! Go and look for it yourself."

Mr Stamp-About went home, thinking hard. Hallo *had* come to see him. Yes, he certainly *had* been pleased about the ripe plums on that tree – but they had been high up and he couldn't reach them. But he had taken in a nice dishful for dinner. How had he got them? Of course – he had knocked them down WITH HIS STICK!

And when Mr Stamp-About went into his garden, there was his stick, hanging meekly on a branch of the plum tree, exactly where he had left it. Oh dear, oh dear. Mr Stamp-About

took it down, tiptoed into the house and put it into the hall-stand. His wife called to him.

"Did you find your stick, dear? Where is it?"

"In the hall-stand," said Mr Stamp-About in such a meek voice that Mrs Stamp-About was really astonished. She went out into the hall to ask him more questions about his stick. But he had vanished. Yes – he had slipped out to the bottom of the garden, where he was very, very busy.

But I have a feeling it won't be in that hall-stand tomorrow, because he'll lend it to somebody else and then the trouble will start again!

Caterpillars'
Party

The big moth sailed down to where the five caterpillars were busy eating their dinner. They were fat caterpillars, each with a fur coat on, and they ate very fast indeed.

"Hallo!" said the big moth. "We moths are giving a party for you caterpillars tomorrow night. Would you like to come?"

"A party!" said the biggest caterpillar. "Yes, of course we'd like to come, but why are you giving a party for *us*?"

"Well," said the moth, waving his beautiful feelers about. "I don't expect you know it, but one day *you* will be moths like us! And we thought we would give a party for you, and tell you how to behave when the time comes for you to be moths."

The furry caterpillars were astonished. "How can we change into moths?" they said. "We have no wings. We are covered with fur. We are quite different from you!"

"I dare say!" said the moth. "But all the same, my words will come true. You see if they don't! Well, what about this party?"

"We'd love to come!" said the caterpillars at once.

"Well, come to the big bush over there tomorrow night when the moon is full," said the moth. "Look out for

41

the hedgehog, though, if he's about. He likes a meal of grubs as fat as you!"

Off flew the moth, his powdery wings taking him high in the air. He was a beautiful thing. The caterpillars watched him go. Could it be true that one day they would be as lovely as that, and fly through the air?

A small pixie came wandering by. The caterpillars called to him eagerly. "Tippy! We're going to a party!"

"Really?" said Tippy. "Well, mind you go nice and clean, with your coats gleaming. Everyone has to look his best at a party."

He skipped off. The caterpillars looked at one another. "Do we look nice enough to go to a party? Ought we to dress ourselves up or something? The moths do look so beautiful."

Now that night there came a great rainstorm. The enormous raindrops

battered the plants on which the caterpillars fed, and broke them. The frightened creatures found themselves on the ground in the mud. They squirmed here and there, but they couldn't get away from the rain.

"What a mess we are in!" said one, sadly. "All covered with mud – and our fur dirty and wet. We can't possibly go to the party."

They looked at one another. They certainly were in a dreadful mess. No party for them! Why, the moths would turn them away in disgust.

And just then who should come by again but Tippy the pixie. They called to him dolefully. "Tippy! See what the rain has done to us! We can't go to the party."

43

Tippy looked at the wet, muddy, untidy caterpillars. He scratched his head and thought hard. Then he spoke. "Caterpillars, I could clean you and tidy you up, if you like – but you would have to give me a reward."

"Just say what you would like and if we can give it to you, you shall have it," said the caterpillars eagerly. "But don't ask for gold, because we don't even know what it is, unless it is the sunshine that shines each day, and you have plenty of that yourself."

"I'll tell you what I want," said Tippy. "I want your fur coats! I could clean them, and make them into fur rugs to sell to the pixies to put on their beds in the winter-time."

There was a most astonished silence. Then the biggest caterpillar spoke in a shocked voice. "What! Give you the fur coats we wear? Why, they *grow* on us! We couldn't possibly do that."

Tippy grinned. "Well, listen – suppose a time comes when you really don't want your hairy coats – when

44

you want to throw them away – will you give them to me then? I promise not to ask you for them unless you say you don't want them."

"All right," said the biggest caterpillar, cheering up. "That's a bargain. You get us all nice and tidy for the party – and we'll let you have our fur coats if we don't want them."

So Tippy set to work on the hairy caterpillars. He fetched his little sponge. He dipped it into a little pool of dew and wetted it. Then he sponged

each muddy caterpillar very carefully to get off the mud. Soon their fur coats were quite clean again.

"Now you are very wet," said Tippy. "Sit out here in the sun – it's just rising, look – and see if you can get really warm and dry."

So out they all sat. Tippy watched them. Then he fetched his little brush, and began to brush the caterpillars' soft, dry hairs.

"Beautiful!" said Tippy, brushing away hard. "It's a pity there's no time to curl your hairs a bit. You'd look fine. There now – that's the last one of you done. Your fur coats have never looked nicer. Stay in the sun today, and towards evening I'll give you one more brushing."

When the caterpillars went to the moths' party they looked very neat and tidy indeed. Tippy had even parted their hairs down the middle, and

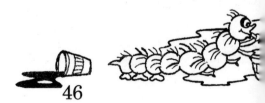

squirted a little of his best scent on them. The moths thought they looked very fine indeed.

The party was lovely. There was plenty to eat, and the dew-drinks were all flavoured with honey that the moths had drawn from flowers with their long tongues. They told the caterpillars many interesting things, half of which the long-bodied creatures could not believe.

"They said we would go to sleep for a long time and wake up as moths," said the fattest caterpillar, on his way home. "What nonsense!"

"And they said that although we should go to sleep as caterpillars, with heaps of legs, a long body, and no wings, we should wake up with only six legs, some fine feelers, a short body, and two pairs of wings!" said another caterpillar. "Impossible! Such things don't happen."

They told all these things to Tippy when they next saw him. He laughed.

"Well, you never know," he said. "There is plenty of most peculiar magic in the world, you know. But before you go to sleep, and change into moths, I want those fur coats of yours! It's about time I had them, too. You eat so much, caterpillars, that I am sure you will burst your skins soon!"

The caterpillars certainly were eating a lot – and some of them were so fat they looked as if they might burst at any moment. Then the biggest one suddenly stopped eating.

"I feel strange," he said. "Very strange. My skin is too tight for me. It's splitting! It is, really!"

48

Pop! It split down his back. "I must get out of my skin!" cried the caterpillar. "It's too tight. It's too tight! Help me, Tippy!"

Tippy helped him. The caterpillar wriggled and Tippy tugged. Soon the tight skin was peeling away from the caterpillar's body. It was off! There it lay beside him, a little ball of fur, a tiny fur-coat that he no longer wanted.

"You've got a beautiful new hairy skin underneath!" said all the other caterpillars, staring. "What a wonderful thing!"

"Of course he has!" said Tippy. "I've seen caterpillars doing this for years!

49

Hurry up and split your coats, you others. I want the skins to make into fur rugs. Don't forget your bargain with me."

Well, of course, the other caterpillars soon got so fat that their skins split too, and you should have seen Tippy pulling and tugging at them, and the caterpillars wriggling. Soon the pixie had a fine hoard of furry skins in his cottage. The caterpillars were only too pleased to let him have them. They all had beautiful new furry coats, under their old skins!

And dear me, those coats split too as soon as the caterpillars grew too fat for them! Tippy was always there when that happened, you may be sure, and he rolled up the cast-off fur coats, put them on his shoulder, and marched off with them.

One day the caterpillars could eat no more. They began to weave themselves silken beds, and they went to sleep inside these. They were too sleepy even to say goodbye to Tippy.

But he said goodbye to them. "I'll see you when you wake up!" he said. "And you'll see what a fine little shop I have then, with fur rugs of all kinds hanging up for sale!"

He was soon very busy. He cut each furry coat and trimmed it so that it made an oblong rug. He washed each one carefully and set it to dry in the sun. Then he brushed the fur well.

After that he hired a tiny shop and hung up the rugs for sale. The very small ones were for the pixie cots or

51

prams. The bigger ones were for beds. And how the little folk hurried to buy them!

"Such beautiful rugs! As warm as can be! Wherever did Tippy get them? Tippy dear, what fur is this? What animal gave you his skin for these lovely rugs?"

But Tippy wouldn't tell his secret. No, he wasn't going to have anyone sharing such a fine secret!

One day the caterpillars in the silken cocoons woke up. They crawled out of their cosy beds and looked round. They stared at one another in surprise.

"We're different! We've got wings! We're moths!"

So they were. They spread their soft, powdery wings and flew off into the night air, rejoicing. It had been nice to be greedy caterpillars – but oh, how much nicer to be moths, with wings like the little folks, and with a long tongue that could pierce to the heart of a flower and drink the sweet nectar hidden there!

They went to see Tippy. He showed them his fine collection of fur rugs. "See?" he said. "You didn't want them but I did! They will keep many a pixie and elf warm in the winter nights. How different you look, moths! Magic has been at work on you – powerful magic!"

It's strange, isn't it, that caterpillars throw away their coats when they grow too big for them? Have you ever found one, rolled up and cast away? Perhaps Tippy has been before you and taken each one. Clever little thing, isn't he?

The Toys
Go On Strike

"Will you stand up!" cried Betty to Amanda, her doll. "You're a very bad, disobedient girl! You just *won't* stand up!"

It wasn't surprising that Amanda wouldn't stand up, because she couldn't. She was a sit-down doll, and she sat down beautifully. But she couldn't bend her legs straight to stand up.

Betty slapped her hard, then threw her into a corner. Amanda fell on her face, and a little bit was chipped out of her pretty nose.

"My train is just as annoying as your doll," said Tom. "These carriages have got so locked together that I can't see how to undo them. Bother them!"

He tugged and pulled so roughly that he broke the little hooks that joined the carriages together. Then, when he tried to set his train properly on the rails, the carriages couldn't be joined at all, because the hooks and loops were broken.

Tom kicked his train and it fell over on its side. Then he stamped on one of the rails. He was in a very bad temper. He looked about for something else to do. He saw his box of bricks and kicked that round the room, too, so that the bricks flew here, there and everywhere!

"Let's go out!" said Tom. "I hate these silly toys! They really seem to *try* and be stupid!"

"Well, let's hope they will behave themselves this afternoon, when John and Pam come to tea," said Betty. "I've a good mind to put Amanda at the back of the cupboard and not let her come to tea at all. Pretending that she can't stand up!"

The children went out of the room, and soon the toys heard them playing in the garden. Amanda the doll began to cry, because she knew her nose had been chipped.

The monkey spoke up. "Toys! I know we are not supposed to come alive until it's dark – but really, we simply *must* do something about these horrid children! Amanda, stop crying. I'll mend your nose for you."

The monkey fetched a little tube of glue and found the broken chip of china on the floor. He fixed it on Amanda's nose with a spot of glue.

"There!" he said. "You look all right

again. Stop crying, or your tears will unstick the glue. Smile! That's better."

The old teddy-bear spoke loudly and gloomily. "What a pity we belong to children like these! Look at my neck. Betty cut some of my fur off the other day."

"Well, what about *me!*" said the pink cat. "Tom pulled my tail off. There it is, on the floor of the cupboard. I feel cold at the back without my tail and

I'm sure I look dreadful!"

"Look at us all over the floor again, sure to be kicked about and trodden on," said a brick, crossly. "I've got a bit broken off me already. It's a shame. We bricks used to build lovely houses and castles. But nowadays we are only flung about the room and trodden on!"

"Half my hair has gone," said the curly-haired doll, Janet. "It used to be so pretty."

She opened and shut her eyes. She was a very clever doll, for she could not only open and shut her eyes, she could walk, and she could say "Ma-ma" to Betty when a string was pulled at her neck.

"Let's go on strike!" said the monkey suddenly. The toys stared at him.

58

"What does that mean?" asked the bear. "It sounds as if you want us to be matches and strike. I don't want to burst into flames, thank you."

The monkey laughed. "No, it doesn't mean that. When workmen go on strike it means that they stop work and won't do any more till their troubles are put right. It isn't a very noble thing to do – but we might try it with Betty and Tom, just to see if it makes any difference in their behaviour."

"Well – but how can we go on strike?" asked Amanda, puzzled. "We don't do any work."

59

"We won't play with the children any more!" said the monkey. "If they build up the bricks, then the bricks must fall down. If they send the engine round the rails, then it must fall off and refuse to run. If they try to make you shut and open your eyes, Janet, you must shut them and refuse to open them. Clockwork clown, if they wind you up, you mustn't go head-over-heels at all."

"It sounds rather a good idea," said the little clockwork mouse. "If they wind me up, I shall run into a hole and not come out!"

"Splendid!" said the monkey. "Now,

hush! Here come the children back again!"

Mother came in with the children. She made them tidy up the room at once. "Bricks and toys all over the place!" she said. "How badly you treat your lovely toys! I'm ashamed of you!"

Betty and Tom sulked. They put their toys away and then went to wash for dinner. "We'll show Pam how Janet opens and shuts her eyes, and walks and talks," said Betty to Tom. "She hasn't a doll as clever as that!"

"And I'll show John how fast my train goes on its railway lines," said Tom. "He's only got an ordinary train, a wooden one that doesn't wind up."

"And we'll build a very high castle with our bricks," said Betty. "And we'll wind up the clown and make him go head-over-heels a hundred times."

The toys listened. Aha! Betty and Tom could make all the plans they liked. If the toys didn't want to play, they wouldn't.

Pam and John came at three o'clock.

They were two very nice children, with good manners. They were thrilled to see all the toys Betty and Tom had, for they hadn't nearly such nice ones in their own home.

"I'll show you how fast my train goes," said Tom, and he wound up the engine. He fastened as many trucks on as he could, except the ones he had broken that morning. He set a tunnel over the lines. He put the signal near, ready to work the signal arm up and down. "Now you watch!" he said. "My train will go roaring round the track, under the tunnel and past the signal. You just watch. It's marvellous!"

But it wasn't a bit marvellous. First the lines broke here and there and Tom had to put them together again. Then the signal fell over on to the line. Then the tunnel got too near the rails

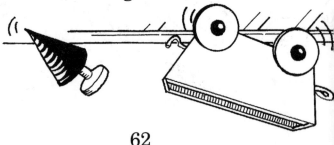

and there wasn't enough room for the train to pass, so it upset the tunnel and stopped.

When everything was put right, the engine ran right off the lines and fell over, its wheels turning fast in the air.

"It doesn't seem a very good railway set you've got," said John. "Everything keeps going wrong. I think I prefer my own wooden train at home. You should see the loads it can carry!"

"Pooh!" said Tom rudely and wound up his engine again. But it ran straight off the rails into his ankle and spilt all its trucks round him! It just would not go! It was on strike!

Then Betty showed Janet, the clever doll, to Pam. "She opens and shuts her eyes, and walks and talks," she said. "Now look."

Janet shut her eyes – but she wouldn't open them! Betty shook her hard, but it wasn't a bit of good! Janet was on strike and wouldn't open her pretty blue eyes. She wouldn't walk either. And instead of saying "Ma-ma" when the string at her neck was pulled she said "Ha-ha!" just as if she was laughing at Betty.

"Stupid doll!" said Betty and threw her down. "I hate her!"

"Don't be so rough with her," said Pam, picking up Janet and rocking her gently. "She's a darling."

Janet opened her eyes at once and looked up at Pam. Pam was delighted. "There! She's opened her eyes for *me*!"

Betty snatched the doll from her. Janet at once shut her eyes and refused to open them.

"She's on strike!" said Pam with a laugh. "She doesn't like you, so she won't do anything for you!"

"Don't be silly," said Betty, but secretly she felt very puzzled. Why wouldn't Janet open her eyes for her and yet open them at once for Pam?

The children began to build with their bricks. Betty and Tom had half and Pam and John had half as well. But no matter how carefully Betty tried to balance her bricks on one another, they fell off with a thud. Neither she nor Tom could build even a wall!

But the bricks behaved very well for Pam and John, and the two built a

65

very fine castle indeed, with tall towers at each end!

"The bricks will build for us, but not for you," said John with a laugh. "You said you hated your doll just now, Betty – well, it almost looks as if your toys hate you!" Nothing went right that afternoon for Betty and Tom. The clockwork mouse was wound up to run across the floor, but instead of that he ran into a real mousehole and wouldn't come out! And the clockwork clown wouldn't turn head-over-heels, even when he was fully wound up. He just wouldn't. He stood there on his

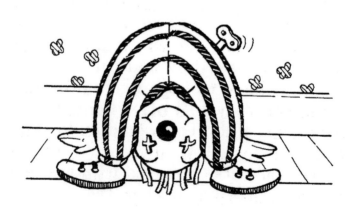

head, but that was all. He wouldn't go over and over.

But as soon as Pam picked him up and set him down on the floor he performed beautifully. "He likes me," said Pam. "But he doesn't like you, Tom. Wind him up again and see if he will somersault for you."

But no, he wouldn't. Tom went red and felt angry. John wouldn't let him slap the clown or throw him down. "No, don't be rough and unkind," he said. "Nearly all your lovely toys are chipped or spoilt or broken in some way. No wonder they won't do anything for you!"

Even their ball bounced away out of the window when Tom picked it up! Nothing would play with them at all. It really was very odd.

"We'll have to go now," said Pam, when the visit was over. "Thank you for having us. And do be nice to your toys in future. I'm sure they're all on strike. I should be very ashamed if my toys wouldn't play with me!"

67

Tom stared at Betty when they were alone again. "Funny, isn't it, Betty?" he said. "It really does seem as if our toys are on strike."

"We shouldn't have been so horrid and impatient with them!" said Betty, almost in tears. "Let's be nicer. It was awful when our toys wouldn't do anything for us – but all kinds of things for Pam and John!"

"All right. We'll be nicer and see if the toys stop striking!" said Tom. "But I'm sure they won't!"

The clockwork mouse suddenly ran out of the hole and raced across the floor to Tom. The clown began turning head-over-heels at once. Janet opened her eyes, looked at Betty and said "Mama" quite clearly!

"Look at that!" said Tom. "I believe the toys must have heard what we said. And look – my engine is making a whirring noise. I believe it wants to show me that it can go round the rails without rushing off them!"

He put it on the rails and it rushed round and round most beautifully without once falling off. "There you are!" said Tom. "It's quite all right now. The toys aren't on strike any more. And I hope they never will be again."

Well, they won't if Betty and Tom keep their word. Have *your* toys ever been on strike? I hope not!

The Boy Whose Toys Came Alive

There was once a boy called Sammy, who longed for his toys to come alive.

"I'm sure you come alive at night and have a lovely time!" Sammy said to them. "Well, why can't you come alive and really play with me in the daytime? Oh, I do wish you would!"

But they didn't – until something peculiar happened. It was like this. Sammy was walking along the lane to his home when a tiny rabbit flung itself out of the hedge and crouched down at Sammy's feet. After the rabbit came a fierce little weasel.

Sammy was frightened – but he picked up the little rabbit and held it safely in his arms. "You go away!" he said to the weasel. Just as he spoke a small brownie came running from the hedge, smacked the weasel sharply on the back, and ran up to Sammy.

"Oh, you've saved my pet rabbit for me!" he cried. "Thank you a thousand times, Sammy! Snowball escaped this morning from her hutch, and I knew the weasel would be after her. Come here, you silly little Snowball!"

Snowball leapt from Sammy's arms into the brownie's. The little man petted and scolded her. Then he spoke to Sammy.

"I do feel so grateful to you for saving my pet rabbit. Is there anything I can do for you in return?"

Well, you can just guess what Sammy thought of at once! His toys!

"Yes, there is something you can do

for me," he said. "Make all my toys come alive! Can you do that?"

"Yes, I can," said the brownie. "But just tell me this first – are you a good boy or a naughty one?"

"Does that matter?" asked Sammy, going red. He was a naughty boy, not very kind to others, often disobedient, and so noisy that his mother was always having headaches.

"Well, it does matter a bit," said the brownie. "You see, your toys will behave like *you* when they come alive. It wouldn't do to have a nursery full of bad toys, you know. You'd get very tired of them. Also, you must promise not to tell anyone they are alive."

"Of course I promise!" said Sammy. Then he told a story. "I'm a good boy!" he said. "So do make my toys come alive!"

"Very well," said the brownie. He felt in his pocket and brought out a little tin. "Rub this yellow ointment on to your toys," he said. "It will make them all come alive."

Sammy was so excited that he forgot to say thank you. He tore off home with the tin and rushed up to his playroom. Which toy should he make come alive first?

"I'll make my clown come alive!" he said. So he rubbed a little of the ointment on to the clown's face. It acted like magic! The clown yawned, got up and ran round the nursery at once! Sammy could hardly believe his eyes. This was simply fine!

"Come here, clown," he said. "I want to have a look at you. Come and speak to me."

73

"Don't want to," said the clown, "I want to play with the bricks."

"Come here at once when I tell you!" said Sammy angrily. Do you know, that clown turned and made a very rude face at Sammy!

Sammy was so angry that he ran after him and slapped him hard. And that naughty little clown turned round and pinched Sammy in the leg! Then he ran off and got behind the toy-cupboard so that Sammy couldn't reach him.

"All right, you just wait!" said Sammy. He went to where he had left his tin of ointment and picked it up. He rubbed some on to his soldiers, his teddy-bear, his sailor-doll, his train, his horse-and-cart, his red ball, and his bricks!

Well, you should have seen the playroom after that! The soldiers at once began to march in splendid rows, and the soldier band began to beat the drum and blow the trumpets! It sounded beautiful.

The teddy-bear chased the sailor-doll, and the train shot round the playroom so fast that it bumped into the box of bricks. But the bricks were alive and sprang out of their box at once. They hopped about, and threw themselves here and there joyfully. One brick threw itself at the teddy-bear and hit him on the nose. The bear was angry and ran after all the bricks, which hopped about the floor like mad things, making a tremendous noise!

"Stop that noise!" said Sammy, who was afraid his mother would come in.

But do you suppose those bricks stopped? Not a bit of it! They danced about all the more, and two of them threw themselves at Sammy and hit him on the head!

Then the train got excited and ran over Sammy's foot. Its key caught his ankle and hurt him. Sammy held his foot and hopped about in pain.

"He thinks he's one of the bricks hopping about!" cried the sailor-doll rudely. "Just look at him!"

Sammy bent down and slapped the sailor-doll – and the doll gave a howl of rage, ran to the work-basket on the window-seat, took out a needle and pricked Sammy in the leg with it.

"Ow! Ow-ow!" yelled Sammy, hopping round again, first on one foot and then on the other. How his toys laughed!

Then the horse-and-cart began to gallop round the playroom – and you should have seen the horse kick up its little wooden legs! And how it neighed too! Sammy would have loved to listen if only it hadn't made quite such a noise!

"You do make a noise," he grumbled. "Oh, goodness me – now that ball's begun bouncing itself! I say, don't bounce so high, ball! Do you hear me? Don't bounce so high!"

The ball squeaked for joy and went on bouncing just as high as it wanted to. It bounced so high that it struck a vase of flowers – and over went the flowers, and down went the vase on to the floor, crash!

Well, all this noise was really too

much for Sammy's mother. She was resting downstairs, and she called up to Sammy, "Sammy! Come here! What was that you broke just now?"

Sammy went down to his mother, looking cross and worried. "I didn't break anything," he said. "The ball bounced up and knocked down the vase of flowers."

"Oh, Sammy, that was very naughty of you," said Mother.

"Mother! I didn't do it!" cried Sammy. "It was the ball, I tell you."

"Don't talk like that," said his mother. "And don't be silly. Balls don't bounce themselves."

But that was just what Sammy's ball *was* doing, wasn't it! Sammy went back upstairs, very cross and upset.

"Here he comes! Here he comes!" he

heard his toys say as he came in at the door. They were all waiting for him.

The ball bounced up into his face and hit his nose. The bricks, which had built themselves up into a high tower, made themselves fall all over him. The clown pinched his left leg and the teddy-bear pinched his right one. The sailor-doll pulled his laces undone. The train tried to run up his leg. The horse galloped his cart over Sammy's left foot and back again in a most annoying way, and all the soldiers ran at him and tried to poke through his socks with their guns and swords.

"What are you all doing, you bad toys?" cried Sammy.

The toys danced round in glee, shouting and squealing.

"You were never kind to us!" yelled

the bear. "We're having fun now you've made us come alive!"

And then the clown did a silly thing. He saw the tin of yellow ointment where Sammy had left it on the chair – and he ran to get it.

"I'm going to make the chairs and tables come alive!" he yelled. "Watch me, toys!"

And then, to Sammy's horror, that naughty clown ran to the table and rubbed some yellow ointment on to its legs. Then he rubbed some on to the chairs and then smeared some on the cushions, the fender, the stool, the lamp and everything else he could think of!

"Stop, stop!" shouted Sammy. But it was too late – the whole of the playroom was alive!

Goodness, you never heard such a noise as that furniture made! The table at once began to dance round and round, first on one leg and then on the other. The chairs played "Catch" with one another, and banged all round the

room trying to grab each other with their legs.

The lamp tried to get out of their way and bumped into the stool, which was very angry and kicked the lamp so hard that it made a dent in it.

The fender began to laugh and stood itself up on end to see how tall it was. All the cushions rolled off the chairs, and tried to flop on top of the toys.

Sammy stood by the wall, looking quite frightened. It was like a bad dream. The armchair raced by and bumped into him. Sammy fell down at once, and all the other chairs raced over him. The fender laughed so much that it fell down with a crash.

"This is awful," said Sammy, trying

to get up out of the way of the stool, which seemed to think it would like to stand on Sammy's middle. The fender stood itself up again to see better. A large blue cushion flung itself on top of the surprised teddy-bear, and he sat down hard, with a growl. The fender laughed so much that it fell down again.

"*Silly* fender. Stupid fender!" said Sammy, feeling very angry with it. "Stop laughing!"

But the fender couldn't. Then the train began to laugh too – the engine, the carriages, and the rails – and they made such a noise skipping about and

squealing, that Sammy felt quite certain his mother would be angry enough with him to send him to bed for the rest of the day.

"Listen, toys! Listen, everyone," said Sammy, trying to make them stop. "I shall get into such trouble if you behave like this! I never knew such a noisy, disobedient nursery! Wherever in the world do you get these bad manners from?"

"You!" screamed the toys. "We've learnt it all from watching *you*! That's why we're noisy! That's why we're rude and disobedient! That's why we're unkind! You taught us!"

The clock on the mantelpiece suddenly struck twenty-one without stopping and walked up and down like a policeman. The fender began to laugh again, and down it fell with a crash.

This time it fell on the clown, who was so hurt that he yelled the place down.

"Stop screaming like an express

train!" cried Sammy angrily. "I know you'll bring my mother up here! Oh, how I wish I'd never made you come alive, you tiresome things!"

"Well, we *are* alive, so you'll have to put up with it!" said the teddy-bear rudely.

"If you talk to me like that I'll smack you!" shouted Sammy. He ran to smack the bear, and the fender stood itself up again to see the fun. But before Sammy could smack the teddy, the clown neatly tripped him up and down he went with a bang. The fender almost choked with laughing and fell down with a worse crash than usual.

Sammy kicked the fender. He kicked the stool. He kicked the engine and the red ball. He kicked everything he could reach, for he was in a terrible temper.

And then the toys and everything else decided that they would do a little kicking too. After all, if you are a table with four legs, you can do a lot of kicking! So they all rushed after Sammy, and the table got four fine

kicks in all at once. Sammy gave a yell and rushed out of the room.

"After him, after him!" shouted the table, and tried to get through the door. But it got mixed up with the fender, who was hopping along to see the fun, and it was a good half-minute before they got outside the door. Then the fender laughed so much that it fell down again, and the table jumped over it and left it there on the landing.

Now Sammy had rushed to his room and locked the door, but the nursery-things didn't know this. They thought he had run downstairs. So down they all went, helter-skelter, after him. Well, really, you never heard such a noise!

The table clattered down on all four legs, and the chairs jumped two stairs at a time. The coal scuttle rolled itself down and made a great noise. The stool hopped down, and the cushions rolled over and over. The fender stopped laughing, and slid itself down, bump-bump-bump, from stair to stair. It was enjoying itself thoroughly.

The clown and the rest of the toys

rushed down after the furniture. They all had to pass the open door of the room where Sammy's mother was trying to rest.

She saw the table gallop past, and she was most astonished. She thought she must be dreaming.

Then the chairs hopped by, and Sammy's mother sat up and stared. Then the lamp rolled by and the stool trotted along behind.

"I must be mad!" thought Sammy's mother. "Am I really seeing tables and chairs running along? Why are they running along? Where are they going? Oh dear, it really makes me feel ill!"

The fender came along and stared in at the room. When it saw Sammy's mother looking so frightened it began to laugh, and down it fell with such a

crash that Sammy's mother nearly leapt off the sofa. The fender picked itself up and hopped on after the others. Then the toys raced along too, and the engine clattered by with its carriages. The ball bounced along and the bricks hopped gaily. It was really an alarming sight.

Sammy was trembling in his bedroom. He heard everything racing by, and he wondered what his mother would say if they all went into her room – and then he heard them out in the garden! He went to his window and looked out.

"Where's he gone?" cried the clown.

"He must be down the lane!" growled the teddy-bear.

"After him!" shouted the lamp – and out of the garden gate they all went.

Well, they made such a noise that the brownie who lived in the lane peeped out to see what it was all about. And when he saw the live toys and furniture, he guessed at once what had happened.

"They must belong to Sammy – and he used his yellow ointment on them!" he cried. "Oh my, he must have been a bad boy to have such noisy, naughty toys! I shall have to do something about this!"

He ran into the lane and spoke to the toys and the furniture.

"What's all this? What's all this?

Please walk by me, one by one, slowly and without noise."

Everything was afraid when they heard the brownie's stern, rather magical voice. So one by one they went quietly by him – and quickly he dabbed each toy and each piece of furniture with a blue ointment.

When every one of them had gone by, the brownie called to them sternly. "In two minutes you will no longer be alive. You had better go quietly back to Sammy's playroom unless you want to be left out in the lane."

What a shock all the toys and the furniture got! They were so afraid of being left out of doors that they all turned round and rushed up the lane, through the gate, and into the house. And Sammy's mother saw them all again, rushing the *other* way this time!

"I'm dreaming again!" she said. "Oh dear, I must be ill or something. And here's that dreadful fender staring at me again, and laughing!"

Sure enough the fender began to

laugh, and it laughed so much that when it fell down with a crash at the bottom of the stairs, it couldn't get up again. And the two minutes were up before it could climb the stairs, so there it stayed, quite still.

But all the other things got safely into Sammy's playroom and just had time to arrange themselves in their places before the magic worked. They gave a sigh, and stayed as still as could be. There wasn't a growl from the teddy nor was there a creak from a chair!

When everything was quite quiet, Sammy unlocked his door and peeped out. He tiptoed to his room. He saw that everything was quite still. He wondered if he could possibly have dreamt it all – but no, there was the little tin of yellow ointment still on the chair.

"Horrid stuff!" cried Sammy. He picked up the tin, put on the lid, and then threw it as far as ever he could out of the window!

"If my toys behave like me, then I must be a very bad boy!" thought Sammy to himself. "I'll try and be a bit better in future. Oh, goodness – here's Mother! I'm sure she will be cross with me."

Sammy was right – she was! She had made up her mind that Sammy must have thrown all the furniture and toys downstairs and then thrown them up again!

"What a bad, naughty boy you are, Sammy!" she said. "What do you mean by throwing everything downstairs? And do you know you've left the fender at the bottom of the stairs and I nearly fell over it! You will go straight to bed and stay there."

"Yes, Mother," said poor Sammy, trying to be good and obedient for once. He went to his room, but on the way he peeped down the stairs and saw the fender at the bottom.

"You can stay there!" said Sammy. "Laughing like that! I suppose you thought it was all very funny!"

The fender tried to laugh but it couldn't. Sammy went to bed, very sad and sorry.

And so far nobody has found that tin of ointment yet. But if you do (it's a very bright yellow), just be careful how you use it. You don't want to end up in bed like Sammy!

93

"I Dare You To!"

"I dare you to!" said Geoffrey to Bill.

The two boys were standing outside old Mr White's cottage. It had a funny old-fashioned bell-pull, and when you pulled the handle you could hear a bell jangling somewhere in the little house.

"Go on – pull it! I dare you to!" said Geoffrey. He was always daring somebody to do something silly – and nearly all the boys were silly enough to take his dares.

"Pooh – I would dare a lot more than just pulling a bell!" said Bill, scornfully. He ran up to the front door and gave the bell-rope a terrific pull. To his horror it came away in his hand, and at the same time there was a loud jangling noise inside the house.

"Run!" shouted Geoffrey. "You've broken the rope, you idiot! Run!"

Bill ran for all he was worth. Old Mr White was a hot-tempered fellow, and he was getting very tired of mischievous children who tugged at his bell-pull. Whatever would he say to somebody who broke it?

Bill fled down the street, feeling ashamed of himself for running away. But that afternoon, when Geoffrey told the other boys how Bill had taken his dare, and not only pulled at old Mr White's bell but had actually tugged the rope in two, Bill found himself quite a hero! He forgot that he had been ashamed of running away, and he began to boast.

"That was nothing! I'd take a bigger dare than that!"

"I dare you to ride down Langham Hill without your bike brakes on!" said Geoffrey at once.

"Right!" said Bill.

"Don't be such an ass," said Derek, the head-boy of the class. "You'll have an accident. That hill is too steep to ride down without brakes on."

"There's hardly any traffic down that hill," said Bill. "I shan't have an accident, don't worry. I've got all my wits about me. It'll be great sailing down there at top speed."

The boys all went to see him take the dare and ride down Langham Hill. It really was a very steep hill indeed, but perfectly straight, and had a good level stretch at the end. Very little traffic used it, because it was too steep.

It certainly looked quite safe.

"Here goes!" said Bill, and got on his bike.

Whoooooooosh! Down he went, twenty miles an hour, thirty, forty . . .

"As fast as a motor-bike!" said the boys, admiringly. "Look at him!"

Bill sped down the hill, enjoying the wind in his hair and the swiftness of his bicycle. What a ride! He came up on the level stretch and the bicycle sped along there too, and then gradually slowed down.

Bill leapt off and waved to the boys who were now running down the hill towards him. Then he rode to meet them, pedalling leisurely along.

"Jolly good!" said Geoffrey. "What did it feel like?"

"Grand," said Bill. "I'd do it again any time. Anyone want to dare me again?"

"We'll think of another dare for you, not the same one," said Geoffrey. "There's nobody as brave as you, Bill."

"And nobody as silly!" thought Derek, the head-boy, but he didn't say it out loud. Bill was so pleased with all the back-thumpings and praise he was getting that he certainly wouldn't like being called silly.

Well, that was the beginning of many other dares. Bill was dared to ride home one night without lights, and he did, though he met the policeman and was rather scared when he was shouted at.

He rode all the way home from school holding on to the tail of a van because Geoffrey dared him to. The van-man saw him and yelled at him, but Bill wasn't going to spoil his dare, and he didn't lose hold of the van till

he came to the road where he lived. Ha – he'd show the boys how brave he was. He was Dare-devil Bill, afraid of nothing.

Certainly Bill was a very clever cyclist. He was always in perfect control of his bicycle, which was a real beauty. It had cost nearly one hundred pounds, and had been a very special birthday present from his mother and father and grandmother. Its brakes were perfect, its lamp was beautiful, and its red rear-light always shone out splendidly.

Bill could ride so slowly on it that it

almost looked as if he were going to fall off, but he never did. He could ride sitting on the saddle, with his feet up on the handlebars to steer instead of his hands. There was no end to the tricks he could do.

"There aren't many dares left for Dare-devil Bill," said the boys at last. "He's done everything."

"I bet he wouldn't dare to ride across the traffic lights when they showed red," said Harry. "Nobody would dare to do that."

"Nobody would be idiotic enough," said Derek.

"Hi, Bill!" shouted Geoffrey. "I've got another dare for you. Would you dare to ride against the traffic-lights – go across when they show red instead of green?"

"You bet!" said Bill at once. "That's easy. Which traffic lights? Choose difficult ones, or it will be no fun."

"All right. Ride over the crossing at the end of the High Street," said Geoffrey. "On the way home from morning school. We'll watch! I bet you'll be nippy enough to get over before anyone knows what you're doing."

Bill was there at the High Street crossing, after morning school, standing with his bike, waiting for the lights to turn red. The boys stood a little way off, watching. Many people were walking up and down the pavement – women shoppers, hurrying men, and small children on their way home to dinner. None of them guessed what Bill was going to do.

The lights turned red against him. Bill leapt on his bike. He rode straight across the road against the lights, with cars hooting at him and drivers

shouting. He was nippy. He kept his wits about him as usual. He was soon at the other side, perfectly safe, and he sailed off into a side-street, in case by any chance a policeman had seen him riding against the lights.

He didn't hear a crash behind him. He didn't hear screams. He didn't see the crowd that gathered round a little girl on the ground. He rode home whistling cheerfully, thinking what a clever, courageous fellow he was.

He went to school that afternoon as usual, expecting to be praised for his daring and patted on the back. He

looked for Geoffrey – but Geoffrey wasn't there. He looked at the other boys and grinned cheerfully. But nobody grinned back. The boys looked away from him. Nobody spoke to him.

"What's up?" said Bill, puzzled.

"Haven't you heard what's happened?" said Derek. "When you rode across the road, against the lights, a car jammed on its brakes so as to avoid you – and it swung across the pavement and knocked down a little girl. She was taken to hospital."

Bill went white. "Who was it?" he said, almost in a whisper. "Anyone I know?"

"Yes. It was Geoffrey's little sister, Bets," said Derek. Then he burst out angrily at Bill.

"You and your idiotic dares! You

think you're so clever, don't you, showing off all the stupid things you can do, breaking all the rules of the road, and getting off scot-free yourself! Look at you – thinking you're so wonderful – and that poor little Bets dying in hospital! You're a worm – no, you're even worse than a worm."

Bill sat down suddenly. He felt ill. Bets – little Bets dying in hospital – why, she had only come to tea the day before yesterday, and he had shown her how to do a jigsaw puzzle. He was fond of Bets, with her round red face and golden curls.

"It isn't true," said Bill with a groan. "Say it isn't true."

"It *is* true," said Derek. "That's why

Geoffrey isn't here this afternoon. He's at the hospital with his mother and father. Imagine what he feels like! It's all because he dared you to do that silly trick that this awful thing has happened to his sister. But you're all right – nothing's happened to *you*! You can still go on taking silly dares, and doing idiotic things, and bringing trouble to other people."

"Don't," said Bill, feeling sick.

"We're all to blame," said Harry. "We all enjoyed seeing him take the dares – and we patted him on the back like anything. We should have smacked his head instead. Poor little Bets! I keep thinking of her. She – she was right under the car, and she screamed."

Bill got up, looking as white as a sheet. He went straight to the headmaster's study and walked in without knocking. The headmaster looked up.

"Sir," said Bill, "I'm in great trouble. It's about Geoffrey's little sister, Bets. Please, sir she's not dying, is she?"

"I don't know," said the Head. "She's badly hurt. I can only hope it wasn't one of the boys of this school who rode against the lights and caused the accident."

"I was the boy," said Bill clutching at the desk. "What shall I do sir? Tell me what to do. Tell me *some*thing!" The headmaster looked at Bill in horror. He got up and spoke sternly.

"The first thing to do is to report to the police. Come with me."

That was a terrible afternoon. In a dream, Bill went to the police-station and gave all the details of the stupid dare to a stern policeman. He went home, and his mother listened in terror and distress to the tale. His father was telephoned for and came home too.

"Mother, what about Bets? Will she die?" Bill asked desperately.

His father telephoned the hospital. "Bets is out of danger," he said thankfully. "She'll recover – but she has a broken arm and leg besides cuts

106

and bruises. Oh, Bill – how could you do this? What unhappiness you've brought on yourself and us, and little Bets and her family!"

"I can never, never make up to Bets for this," thought Bill. "I must go and see her every day at the hospital. I must take her flowers and toys and dolls, and everything I possibly can. But where can I get the money? I've only about twenty pence."

He got the money. He got a great deal of money.

Because, you see, he sold his magnificent bicycle and spent every penny on Bets. She's better now, though she still limps a little. She loves Bill for being so kind.

Bill can't understand why Bets is fond of him. He thinks she should hate him – and Geoffrey too.

"After all, we nearly killed you between us," he tells Bets. "That was the most terrible afternoon of my life, I can tell you; it's changed me into a different person altogether!"

And a very good thing too! What do *you* think?

The
Very-Long-Tail

There was once a tadpole with a very-long-tail. He lived in the pond with the frogs, the toads, the water beetles, the water-spiders, the stickleback, and many other tadpoles.

And wasn't he proud of his very-long-tail!

It certainly was a long one, much longer than the tails the other tadpoles had. The tadpoles used their tails for swimming about the pond – and as this little tadpole had such a long one, he could get about very fast indeed.

"I don't care about the frogs or the water-beetles!" he cried. "I can always swim away from anyone who wants to catch me and scold me! Why, I even raced the stickleback yesterday, and he can go very fast indeed!"

The other tadpoles grew tired of hearing about the very-long-tail.

"He's always boasting about it," they said to one another. "Let's not take any notice of him. He's tiresome and dull, always saying "Look at my very-long-tail!"

So the tadpoles always swam away when the long-tailed one came near, and wouldn't have anything to do with him. He was cross.

"I ought to be their leader," he thought. "I ought to be their king. There's no doubt about that. I am a better swimmer than any of them. We have no king at all. I ought to be king!"

So he asked the tadpoles to make him their king, but they swam away without listening. Then the long-tailed tadpole swam in a rage to the stickleback. "I ought to be king!" he said. "Look at my long tail, and see how fast I swim. Tell the other tadpoles that I am their king, stickleback."

But the stickleback had built himself a little nest, and would not allow anyone to come near. So he chased away the tadpole, trying to tear him with his spines.

The tadpole swam off to the big water-beetle. "Big black water-beetle, I ought to be king of the tadpoles!" he said. "Don't you think I ought to? Look at my long tail and see how fast I swim. Tell the other tadpoles that I am their king, big black water-beetle!"

"Go away," said the black water-beetle. "You bother me with your silly chatter. You are no more like a king than I am like a queen."

The tadpole swam off, talking to himself in a great temper. Why wouldn't anyone see that he was a really marvellous tadpole, and had a tail twice as long as anyone else? Ah, if only he were king he would make all the other tadpoles obey him, and say they were sorry for not talking to him.

He went to a newt who was lying at the bottom of the pond asleep. The tadpole butted him with his head, and the newt woke up with a jump.

"Don't," he said. "What do you want?"

"I want you to go and tell the other tadpoles that I am king," said the tadpole. "Look at my long tail, and see how fast I can swim. I ought to be king."

"I can't decide a thing like that," said the newt, beginning to go to sleep again. "Go and find Leaper, the big green frog, who is king of the frogs, and ask him to make you king of the tadpoles. It is nothing to do with me."

Well, the tadpole spent a long, long time looking for Leaper. No one seemed to know where he lived. The tadpole swam about day after day, asking for him. He was surprised to find that he had little back legs one day. He had no idea how they had come – but he was very pleased.

"I've back legs now," he thought. "This is marvellous – back legs and a very-long-tail! I *ought* to be king."

Then another day he found that he had front legs as well. How splendid! "Back legs *and* front legs – I am indeed a marvellous tadpole!" he said. "If only I can find Leaper, the green frog, I am quite certain he will let me be king of all the tadpoles!"

After a long time the tadpole did at last find Leaper. He was sitting on the bank of the pond, an old, wise and very big green frog. He blinked his eyes as the tadpole poked his head out of the water.

"Your Majesty," said the tadpole. "I've come to ask you to make me king of the tadpoles. I ought to be king."

"Why?" asked Leaper, with a croak.

"Because of my wonderful long tail," said the tadpole. "It makes me swim *so* fast."

"Show me your long tail," said Leaper. The tadpole turned himself round. Leaper croaked with laughter.

"You have no tail at all," said Leaper. The tadpole turned himself round. Leaper laughed again.

"You have no tail at all!" he said. The tadpole looked behind himself in alarm and surprise. But Leaper was quite right. He had no tail! It had gone!

"Oh! Where has it gone? Who has bitten it off? What shall I do without my tail? Oh, dear, dear Leaper, please make me king of the tadpoles, even though I have lost my tail."

115

"There are no tadpoles in the pond," said the frog and he laughed again. The tadpole was astonished. He at once swam back into the pond, and went to look for his old friends, the wriggling tadpoles.

But Leaper was quite right. There were no tadpoles at all. The little tadpole was most puzzled. Where had they gone? He met the stickleback and asked him.

"See that old piece of wood up there, on the top of the water?" said the stickleback with a grin. "Well, go and ask the creatures sitting there where all the tadpoles have gone. They will tell you."

So the little tadpole went to ask. He climbed on to the piece of wood, and saw dozens of tiny frogs sitting there. He spoke to them politely.

"Please could you tell me where the tadpoles are?" he said. "I can't find them anywhere!"

The little frogs laughed loudly. "*We* were the tadpoles!" they said. "But all tadpoles change into frogs. Do you still want to be king of the tadpoles, silly? Well, you must wait till next year then, when more tadpoles will hatch out of frog-spawn in the pond!"

The tadpole was astonished. He looked at himself in the water – and what a shock he got. He was no longer a tadpole – but a little frog like the rest!

"Yes – your tail has gone like ours, and you have front and back legs," said the tiny frogs. "But let us tell you this, Vain-One. We will not let you be our king, because you are so stupid you didn't know you had changed into a

frog. You thought you were still a tadpole with a very-long-tail!"

Poor little frog! He leapt into the water and swam away. Yes, he had been very stupid; and stupid people should not be kings. Only wise people should lead others.

I know what will happen to him if he goes on being stupid. He will be gobbled up by the first wild duck that goes to the pond! Wise frogs live to be as old as Leaper, but silly ones are always eaten up.

"And that is as it should be," croaks Leaper. "Wisdom should live, and foolishness should die! That is the law of all living things. Croak, croak!"

118

Pimmy is Very Busy

Pimmy was the pixie who lived in Pimmy Cottage at the end of Snapdragon Village. You could tell he was a lazy little fellow because his garden was full of weeds, his windows were dirty, and his gate hung crooked.

Now one day it was very, very windy. Pimmy put on his red hat with the feather in it, and went out. It was a silly hat to wear on a windy day, but Pimmy liked it very much. It was his best hat, and the feather made him feel grand.

The wind saw Pimmy's hat with delight. Whooooo! Just the kind of hat the wind liked to play with! It swept down on Pimmy, swished off his hat, and made it sail high in the air.

"Oh – bother, bother, bother!" cried Pimmy as he saw his lovely hat whirled away. "Come back, hat!"

But the hat didn't. It was enjoying itself. It sailed off, went over a tree, and then came down on the top of the shed in Dame Stern's garden.

"That's a nuisance," said Pimmy, screwing up his nose. "I daren't go and get my hat off Dame Stern's shed without asking her – and she may snap my head off, she's so bad-tempered."

Anyway, he went to ask if he might get it, because he really couldn't bear to lose such a lovely hat. He knocked on Dame Stern's door.

"If it's the baker, leave a loaf of bread on the step!" called a voice.

"It isn't," said Pimmy.

"Well, if it's the paper-boy, bring me the right paper tomorrow, or I'll chase you all the way down the street and back again," said the voice.

Pimmy felt glad he wasn't the paper-boy.

"It isn't the paper-boy," he said. "It's Pimmy. My hat has been blown on to the top of your shed, Dame Stern, and please may I get it?"

"No, you may not," said Dame Stern. "You'll fall off and break your neck."

"I could climb up a ladder all right," said Pimmy politely.

"I haven't got a ladder," said Dame Stern. "But Old Man Stamper has. You might be able to borrow his."

Pimmy went off to Old Man Stamper's house. The old fellow was in his garden, digging. "Please, Mr Stamper, could you lend me your ladder?" said Pimmy. "My hat's blown on top of Dame Stern's shed."

"What a silly hat to have," said Old Man Stamper. "Well – I'll lend you my ladder, but you must do something for me first. You run along to Mother Grumble's and ask her to let me have a little of her cough medicine. My cough's so bad at night."

Pimmy didn't want to go to Mother Grumble's. It was a long way to go, and he was afraid of her. But still, he wouldn't get the ladder if he didn't; and if he didn't get the ladder he'd lose his hat. So he had to go.

He came to Mother Grumble's and knocked at the door. He could hear the old lady grumbling away to someone.

"And if it isn't one thing, it's another. One of my hens got loose this morning, and it pecked up all my lettuces, and then a stray dog came and dug up my carrot-bed, and .."

Pimmy knocked again.

"And now here's someone at the door, just as I've got settled down to have a cup of tea! Really, if it isn't one thing, it's another. Who's at the door? Speak up!"

"Pimmy the Pixie!" called Pimmy.

123

"Please will you give Old Man Stamper some of your cough medicine?"

"Well, if he isn't asking all day long for something or other!" said Mother Grumble. "First it's a pinch of tea, then it's a box of matches, and now it's cough medicine. I haven't got a bottle to put any medicine in. You'd better go and ask the chemist to let you have one he doesn't want, Pimmy. Then I'll give you some."

Pimmy groaned. The chemist lived on the other side of the hill. He set off again and came to the chemist.

"Hallo, Lazy Little Pimmy!" said the chemist, who had once had Pimmy for

an errand-boy and sent him away because he was so lazy. "What do you want?"

"Could you let me have an old medicine bottle for Mother Grumble?" said Pimmy.

"Ah, you want something for nothing, do you?" said the chemist. "No, no – if you want a bottle, you must do something to get it, Pimmy. I don't give something for nothing!"

"Well, what shall I do?" said Pimmy, feeling that he would never get home that day.

"See this parcel?" said the chemist. "Well, you take it to Mrs Flap's for me,

and when you come back you shall have the bottle."

Pimmy set off. Mrs Flap's house was half a mile away. Pimmy wished he had had his shoes mended the week before, as he should have done. There was a hole in one, and the stones kept getting in and hurting his foot.

He came to Mrs Flap's. Nobody answered the door. Pimmy knocked and knocked, more and more loudly. Then the window of the next house flew up.

"What's all this noise? It sounds like a thousand postmen at the door – knock, knock, knock! Mrs Flap's not in. She's out shopping."

"Oh dear," said Pimmy, looking at the angry face of Mr Glum. "I've come so far to bring her a parcel from the chemist."

"Well, I'll take it in for you if you'll do something for me," said Mr Glum. "My dog hasn't been for his walk today, and he's longing for it. My leg's bad and I can't take him. You just take

him round the streets and back again, and when you come back I'll take the parcel in for Mrs Flap. Then you won't need to sit on her doorstep and wait."

"I don't like taking dogs for walks," said Pimmy. "And besides, I'm tired."

Mr Glum looked at him hard. "Ah, you're Lazy Little Pimmy, aren't you?" he said. "*You* wouldn't take a dog for a walk, no matter how hard he begged you, would you? You're too lazy."

He slammed down his window. Pimmy stared at it in despair. Mrs Flap might be hours before she came back from her shopping. He couldn't wait all that time. He would have to take Mr Glum's dog for a walk, even though his legs did feel dreadfully tired.

So he shouted out loudly: "Mr Glum, Mr Glum, I'll take your dog out!"

The front door opened. Mr Glum limped out with a very large dog on a lead. "Here you are," he said. "Take him for a nice run and come back again."

Pimmy took the lead and set off. He meant to go round the corner and sit for ten minutes, and then take the dog home again. But the dog had other ideas.

Pimmy didn't take that dog for a run – it took Pimmy for a gallop! It was a large dog and a strong dog, and a very determined dog. It tore off down the street, and Pimmy was dragged after it.

"Here! Hi! Whoa!" panted Pimmy. But the dog took not the slightest notice. It rushed on like an express train, and Pimmy had to follow it. He ran and he ran, and he panted and he puffed. He had never in his life run so fast.

Then the dog suddenly turned and ran back to sniff an exciting smell. The lead wound itself round Pimmy's legs, and he sat down very suddenly. The dog looked surprised, and sniffed at Pimmy's ear.

"Don't, you horrid dog," panted Pimmy. "What do you mean by rushing off at top speed like that? Don't sniff in my ear – it tickles."

The dog sniffed at Pimmy's nose. Pimmy got up, and the dog at once started off at top speed again. But luckily this time it made for home. Pimmy tore along behind it, almost falling over his own feet.

He got back to Mr Glum's, his face hot and red, his breath coming in such loud pants that Mr Glum heard him before he even saw him. Mr Glum smiled one of his rare smiles.

"I see Scamper has been giving you a good run," he said. "Well, it will do you good, Lazy Little Pimmy. Here, Scamper! Come in. Where is the parcel you wanted me to give to Mrs Flap? Ah, there she is. You can give it to her yourself now."

He shut his door. Pimmy glared at it. So he had taken that dreadful dog out for nothing! He scowled, gave the parcel to Mrs Flap and set off wearily to the chemist's.

"What a long time you've been!" said the chemist. "Lazy as usual, I suppose – just crawled along, didn't you?"

"I've been rushing along at about sixty miles an hour!" said Pimmy, crossly, and he took the bottle the chemist held out to him. "Thank you. If I'd known how many miles I had to run when I took that parcel for you, I wouldn't have done it!" Pimmy took the bottle to Mother Grumble. She got up to fill it, grumbling away as usual. "If it isn't one thing, it's another. No sooner do I sit myself down than up I have to get again for lazy little fellows like you, Pimmy!"

Pimmy took the bottle of cough medicine to Old Man Stamper. The old fellow was very glad to have it. He took a dose at once.

"Could I borrow your ladder, please?" said Pimmy. "You said I could if I brought you some cough medicine."

"Dear me, I'd forgotten," said Old Man Stamper. "There it is, look. Mind you bring it back." Pimmy took the

131

ladder. It was very heavy. He staggered
back to Dame Stern's garden and in at
her gate.

"Oh, you've got the ladder, have
you?" said Dame Stern. "Now you be
careful not to tread on any of my
flower beds, Pimmy!"

Pimmy was very careful. His arms
ached with the heavy ladder and he
was glad to put it against the shed. He
went up. Now at last, at last, he would
get his lovely hat!

But it wasn't there! It was gone!
Pimmy burst into tears.

Dame Stern was surprised. "What's
the matter?" she said. "Oh, of course,
your hat is gone. Yes, I saw it go. The

wind came down and swept it away. I don't know where it went to."

Pimmy cried bitterly. He carried the heavy ladder back to Mr Stamper. Then he went home, still crying. And when he got there, what did he see in his very own garden but his lovely hat, feather and all!

"Oh – who brought you back?" he cried in delight, and put it on. The wind swept round him and shouted in his ear.

"I brought it back here, Pimmy. I was just playing a trick on you, that's all. I brought it back!"

"Oh, you mean, unkind wind!" cried Pimmy. "I've borrowed a heavy ladder and carried it ever so far – I've fetched cough medicine –I've carried a parcel – and I've taken a dog out for a run – all to get my hat, and now it's here! I'm TIRED OUT!"

"Do you good, do you good, Lazy Little Pimmy!" said the wind, and tried to pull his hat off again. "Do you good! Whoooo-ooo-ooo!"

The Tale of
Yah-Boo

Once upon a time there lived in Tick-Tock Village a goblin called Yah-Boo.

This may seem a funny name to you, but it was a good name for him, because he so often shouted "Yah-Boo!" to people.

Yah-Boo was a rude little goblin, with no manners at all. He would bump into people when he met them on the path. He would never take his hat off when he met a lady. And if he didn't like anyone, he always called a rude name after them.

When he met old Wizard Frowny, he waited till he was safely past him, and then turned round and put his hands round his mouth to shout.

"Yah-Boo, old stick-in-the-mud!" he

called. "Yah-Boo, old slow coach!"

Frowny was angry. He had a bad leg and he couldn't walk very quickly, and he thought it very unkind of Yah-Boo to call out after him like that.

Sometimes Yah-Boo would shout after old Mother Tiptap.

"Yah-Boo, old mingy-stingy-tiptap!" he called. "Who never gives a penny to anyone? Yah-Boo, old mingy-stingy-tiptap!"

Old Mother Tiptap was so poor that she hardly ever had a penny for herself. It made her cry to hear Yah-Boo shouting after her like that.

He shouted after little Tiddler too.

135

Tiddler was very small for his age, but he made up for it by working very hard and carrying lots of parcels for other people. But Yah-Boo didn't think of that! He just yelled after him as loudly as he could, whenever he passed him.

"Yah-Boo, Tiny Tiddler! It's a wonder your feet reach the ground when you walk, you're so small! Yah-Boo, tiny mite!"

Now one day Yah-Boo had a great deal of money given to him. His old Aunt Trippy, who was very rich, gave a sack of gold to each of her nephews and nieces – and Yah-Boo got one too.

At once his head became filled full of grand thoughts.

"I shall buy beautiful new clothes! I shall ride in a carriage! I shall wear a hat with an enormous feather in it! I shall make all kinds of grand friends and give some grand parties!"

You might have thought that being rich would make Yah-Boo kinder to everyone. But not a bit of it! It made him very high and mighty indeed, and

he called out after people who were not so well-off as himself, in just the same unkind way as before.

"Yah-Boo!" he said to the old beggar at the roadside. "Your hat's got a hole in it, and your head's coming through! Yah-Boo!"

But it so happened that the old beggar at the roadside wasn't really a beggar. It was the enchanter Big-Head, come to collect a few Kind Smiles and Comforting Words from the people passing by. He wanted these for one of his spells.

So he had dressed himself up as a

beggar, and was busy trying to collect all the Comforting Words and Kind Smiles that he could.

When Yah-Boo came by and yelled rude things at Big-Head, the old enchanter was so angry that he dropped the magic bag into which he had stuffed the Comforting Words and Kind Smiles and it fell down a nearby drain.

Big-Head had to pull up the grating over the drain, and put his hand down into the dirty water there to try and find his bag. But he couldn't.

And all the time Yah-Boo called rude things to him. "Dirty Hands! Fancy

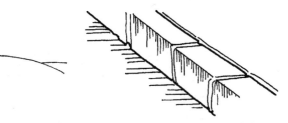

messing about in that muddy water! Nasty old beggar – you'd better fall in the drain yourself, and then we shall be well rid of you! Yah-Boo!"

Big-Head stood up and looked hard at Yah-Boo. The goblin began to feel uncomfortable. He ran away down the street. He would have felt even more uncomfortable if he had known the spell that Big-Head was making for him.

Big-Head was speaking to the wind.

"Follow him, Wind, wherever he goes," said Big-Head, in his deep, soft voice. "Call his name. Make him listen. And tell him things he doesn't want to know. Go, Wind, go. Follow Yah-Boo and talk to him!"

The wind followed Yah-Boo. The goblin was going to his tailor's, to try on a smart new suit. The wind followed him into the shop. It watched him undress and try on the grand suit, which fitted him beautifully.

"I'll wear it home," said Yah-Boo, and he walked out of the shop with his new suit on. It really looked very nice indeed, and Yah-Boo was pleased to see so many people looking at it.

Then the wind's voice spoke loudly to him, calling his name. "Yah-Boo! Yah-Boo!"

"Yes. Yes, who's calling me?" cried Yah-Boo, looking all round. Everyone else looked round too, for the wind had a very loud voice.

"Yah-Boo! You have a hole in your vest!" said the wind, and laughed loudly. "Yes, you have. You are wearing a grand suit, but you have a hole in your vest!"

Yah-Boo went as red as a tomato. He looked down hurriedly to see if his vest was showing. But it wasn't. Who *could* be saying that to him? It was quite true – he *had* got a hole in his vest. How dreadful that everyone should know it!

He walked off, and soon he met Sir Hoppitty and his lady. Yah-Boo was proud to show off his new suit. He stopped and chatted with them. "Yah-Boo!" cried the voice of the wind, sweeping up. "Yah-Boo!"

Yah-Boo took no notice. He was dreadfully afraid that whoever it was would begin to talk.

"YAH-BOO!" roared the wind. Sir Hoppitty looked all round in surprise.

"Someone is calling you, Yah-Boo," he said.

"YAH-BOO!" cried the wind. "You haven't washed behind your ears!"

Oh dear. It was quite true, Yah-Boo hadn't washed behind his ears. He hardly ever did. He had big ears, too, and he should have washed them carefully.

Sir Hoppitty looked at Yah-Boo's ears and turned up his nose. "Good day to you," he said, and walked on with his lady. He didn't want to talk to people who didn't wash behind their ears.

Yah-Boo looked hard all round to see if anyone was hiding anywhere. But he couldn't see who it was that had called out rude things. He went on home, and was glad to be indoors. He put the kettle on to make himself some tea.

He was just making it when Mr Twinkle called in. Mr Twinkle was a smart little brownie, and Yah-Boo was trying to make friends with him.

"Oh, do sit down, Mr Twinkle," said Yah-Boo, politely. "Will you have a cup of tea?"

"Yah-Boo!" called the wind, getting in at the open window. "Yah-Boo!"

The goblin went pale. Where was this awful person who followed him everywhere? He went to the stove and began to make a great noise there. But the wind could make a much bigger noise. It rattled the window-pane and called more loudly: "YAH-BOO! You forgot to feed your poor old cat yesterday! Unkind goblin, aren't you, Yah-Boo!"

Mr Twinkle was shocked. "Did you really forget to feed your cat?" he asked. "She does look rather thin. I hope you are not the kind of person that does things like that, Yah-Boo, because I could never be friends with you if you are."

"Of course I'm not!" said Yah-Boo. "I never forget to feed my cat, or my canary either."

"Oh, Yah-Boo! Yah-Boo is a bad story-teller!" yelled the wind, enjoying itself very much. "Yah-Boo only tells

143

the truth when he wants to. Yah-Boo is a nasty little goblin!"

"I don't like this," said Mr Twinkle, and he got up and went away. "There's something very strange here. Good-bye, Yah-Boo."

Yah-Boo was upset. He went out into the garden to fetch in some clothes from the line. Old Mother Tiptap lived next door, and Yah-Boo saw her picking flowers. He was just about to open his mouth and call out a rude name when the wind spoke first.

"Yah-Boo! You didn't give Mother Tiptap her tablecloth back, when it blew over your wall the other day. Yah-Boo, you are a bad fellow! You've still got that tablecloth!"

This was news to Mother Tiptap. She glared at Yah-Boo, and rapped with her stick on the wall.

"You give it back to me!" she said.

"I haven't got it," said Yah-Boo, sulkily.

"Oh, Yah-Boo is a dreadful story-teller!" cried the wind, blowing over the wall, and taking off Yah-Boo's pointed cap. "He's mean! He's bad! He's rude!"

"Who are you calling rude names?" yelled Yah-Boo. "Where are you?"

"Over the wall!" cried the wind. "I've got your cap! I'm taking it away!"

Yah-Boo saw his cap racing over the wall and into a field. He jumped over the wall and went after it. "There's some imp I can't see going off with my hat!" he said. "I won't have it, I won't!"

He tore after his hat, but the wind took it into a wet, marshy meadow, and Yah-Boo soon found himself up to the waist in mud. He struggled out, looking a dreadful sight, all dirty and muddy.

"My new suit is spoilt!" he said. "Oh, how unhappy I am!"

He walked home, wet, cold and muddy. The wind yelled after him all the way.

"Yah-Boo! What a sight you are! Look at your legs! Look at your hands! You've got mud on your face, and mud on your clothes! Yah-Boo, put yourself in the dustbin when you get home!"

Everyone laughed when they heard what the wind shouted. They thought it was good to hear someone shouting rude things after Yah-Boo.

Yah-Boo went home. He shut all the windows. He bolted all the doors.

"Now, whoever you are, you can't get in!" he said. "I won't have rude

146

things shouted at me. I won't!"

But the wind slid down the chimney and blew the soot all over the hearth. "Yah-Boo!" it cried, in glee. "Here I am again. Yah-Boo, what a nasty, horrid, rude, mean little goblin you are! Can I live with you? It's such fun to call you names. You always enjoyed calling other people names, didn't you? It's fun, isn't it? Let me live with you, Yah-Boo!"

Poor Yah-Boo! He packed his bag and went to catch the very next bus. He meant to go and stay with his old

Aunt Trippy, and get rid of whoever it was that was pestering him so.

But the wind got on the bus with him and travelled all the way, blowing round people's legs and making a terrible draught.

"Yah-Boo!" it whispered. "Yah-Boo! I'm coming with you. I'm here, I'm here!"

His Aunt Trippy couldn't bear to hear the shouting and the yelling. She popped Yah-Boo into an empty dustbin, and clapped the lid on him.

"The wind will soon get tired of blowing around a dustbin!" she said. It did – and poor Yah-Boo soon got tired of sitting *in* the dustbin. But, as the wind said, it was a good place for rubbish!

"Goodbye, Rubbish!" it shouted. "You be good, now, or I'll be back again. Goodbye, Rubbish!"

I don't know if Yah-Boo is still in the dustbin – but I'm quite sure nobody will mind if he is.

Pixie
Mirrors

In Clara's garden, though Clara didn't know it, lived a whole family of curly-headed pixies. They were the prettiest things, as light as thistledown, and as merry as a blackbird in spring.

Everybody liked them. The field-mice who lived in the meadow at the bottom of the garden often asked them to tea, and the larks in the field took them to see their young ones as soon as they were out of the egg.

The meadow pixies asked them to dances, and even the cross old goblin who lived inside the hollow oak tree used to poke his head out and smile at them if he heard the flutter of their small wings going by.

Now whenever they were asked out

to a party, the curly-headed pixies used to dress themselves up in their best blue-and-silver dresses, and brush out their hair till it shone like a golden mist around their small heads.

And then they used to fly to Clara's bedroom window, creep in very quietly, and go to Clara's mirror. It stood on her dressing-table, and was very pretty, for it had flowers all round it.

Each pixie took her turn at looking in to see if her dress was right and her hair was neat. They patted their skirts down, and dabbed at their curly hair, chattering excitedly all the time.

And Clara never knew! She didn't guess that the pixies used her mirror for their own, though once, on a rainy night, she was puzzled to find a whole crowd of tiny muddy footsteps on her clean white dressing-table cover!

"Can it be the cat?" she thought. "No – cats don't have such small feet, nor such pointed toes either. It's very odd."

And then one day a dreadful thing happened. Clara went to put some flowers on her dressing-table, and her hand knocked against the mirror. It fell over, slid off the dressing-table and then fell to the ground with a crash! Bits of broken glass flew round Clara's feet.

"Oh, my goodness! Look at that!" cried Clara in dismay. "My lovely, lovely mirror is broken! Mother, Mother, look what I've done!"

Mother was sad. It had been such a beautiful mirror. "Never mind," she said. "Maybe we can get a new glass fitted into it and then it will be all

right again. But you have broken one
or two of the flowers off too, Clara. I
wonder if those can be mended."

"That's seven years' bad luck for
Clara," said Jane, the daily help,
looking in at the bedroom door.

"Don't be silly, Jane," said Mother.
"Bad luck has nothing whatever to do
with breaking a mirror. It's bad luck to
break a mirror, certainly – but really, I
didn't think you still believed that silly
old tale of seven years' bad luck!"

Jane went away blushing. Clara
swept up the broken bits of mirror and

put them into the dustbin. Mother took the broken mirror to see if it could be mended.

So Clara had no mirror on her dressing-table to tell her if she was neat and tidy.

"Well, it's a good thing no one else uses the mirror but me," thought Clara.

That was just where she was wrong! The curly-headed pixies had a great disappointment when they came along that evening to see if they were looking pretty for a dance that the cross old goblin was giving especially for them. There was no mirror there!

"It's gone!" said one.

"Let's look for it!" said another.

But that wasn't any good, because it just wasn't anywhere in the room at all. The pixies were so busy looking for it that they didn't hear Clara come into the room-and the little girl stood staring in surprise and joy at the twelve tiny pixies flying all round her bedroom!

"Am I dreaming?" she cried. "Or are you real?"

The pixies flew together in a bunch, looking round in fright. Then one of them spoke.

"We are real, of course," she said. "We were looking for your mirror, Clara. We always came to peep in it before we went to a party. But now it's gone."

"It's broken," said Clara sadly. "Did you badly want to see yourselves, Pixies? There is a long mirror in my mother's room. You can peep into that if you like."

"No, thank you," said the pixies at once. "We shouldn't really have let *you* see us, Clara – we would get into trouble if we let a grown-up see us. Oh dear – what are we to do? There is not pond in the garden to look into."

"Shall I tell you something?" said Clara suddenly. "Well, listen. This

afternoon when I went down the garden, it had been raining. And as I passed by the lupin plants, I saw such a pretty sight. One of the lupin leaves had curved its pretty green leaflets upwards, and had caught a bright raindrop just in the middle! I am sure you could find it and use it for a mirror!"

"That *is* an idea!" cried the pixies in delight. "We'll go and find it straight away, Clara."

They flew out of the window. They went to where the blue and pink lupins grew. They had pretty leaves cut up into green fingers and, sure enough, in the centre of one was a bright raindrop, just big enough to make a little mirror for the curly-headed pixies! One by one they looked into it, and patted their hair and arranged their dresses. It was just right for them!

Then a pixie knocked against the lupin leaf and the raindrop rolled out and splashed on to the ground. The little lupin mirror was broken!

But it didn't matter. The pixies had finished with it, and went off gaily to their dance. They had a lovely time, and told everyone about the funny little mirror they had found in the lupins.

156

Clara's mirror was mended and was put back on her dressing-table; but the pixies never used it again, though they often remembered Clara and dropped fresh flowers on to her pillow for her to find.

They asked the lupin leaves to hold the raindrops for them whenever it rained - and that is just what they do. They make beautiful mirrors for the little folk, and are simply lovely to see. You won't forget to look for them, will you, after a rain-shower? You will find those pixie-mirrors gleaming brightly here and there, in the centre of the lupin leaves. Roll one out and see it break on the bed below!

The
Biscuit Tree

Once there was a brownie called Mickle who was very poor. He lived in a tumble-down cottage, and grew potatoes and cabbages in his garden, and nothing else, because it was so small.

But though he was poor he was as kind as could be. If anyone came knocking at his yellow front door begging for a penny, he would shake his head and say, "I haven't even a ha'penny. But you may have a slice of bread, or two or three potatoes."

If anyone wanted help, Mickle would always run to give it. When old Dame Fanny broke her leg, he went in to sweep and dust her cottage every day, and he fed her hens so well that they laid even more eggs than usual.

And when Mr Winkle had his roof blown off in a storm, Mickle took a ladder, and spent the whole day mending Winkle's roof most beautifully.

Most people knew how to reward Mickle for his kindness. They would give him a few biscuits.

Mickle was so poor that he never bought a biscuit for himself. His meals were mostly bread, potato, and cabbage, sometimes with soup for a treat.

And he did love biscuits so much!

"I really don't know which biscuits I love most," he would say. "The ginger-snaps are marvellous – such a lovely taste. And the chocolate biscuits that Dame Fanny makes simply melt in my mouth. And as for those little biscuits with the jam in the middle, well, I could eat them all day long!"

Now one day Mickle had a bit of bad luck. A goat got into his garden and ate all his winter cabbages! And when he went to his sack of potatoes to help himself to one or two, he found that a rat must have told his family about them, for nearly all had disappeared through a hole at one end of the sack!

Mickle could have cried! All his winter greens gone – and most of his potatoes! What was he to live on now?

He went indoors. He had been to help Pixie Lightfoot to dig her garden that day, and she had given him six pat-a-cake biscuits as a reward. He had meant to keep them for Sundays, and eat one each Sunday for six weeks at teatime. But today he was so hungry that he felt he could eat them all!

Now just outside at that very moment was a little beggar-child. Her father was a tramp who was walking through the village. She was ragged and cold, and when she saw the smoke rising from Mickle's chimney she thought it would be very nice just to peep inside the door and look at the fire.

So, as Mickle was about to take a bite from the first biscuit, he saw the door slowly open, and the untidy curly head of the little beggar-child come peeping round the corner!

Mickle stared in surprise. The child

161

smiled and came right in.

"I'm cold," she said. "I saw the smoke coming from your chimney and I wanted to look at a nice, warm fire."

"Come and sit down by it," said Mickle at once. "It's only made of sticks from the woods, but it is cheerful and warm."

So the little ragged girl sat down and warmed her hands. She looked at the bag that Mickle was holding and asked him what was inside it.

"Biscuits," said Mickle.

"Ooh!" said the beggar-child, but she didn't ask for one. Her eyes grew rounder, and she looked small and hungry. Mickle felt that he simply *must* give her a biscuit. So he handed her one.

"Thank you!" said the girl, and crunched it up as quickly as a dog eats a bone! Then she looked hungrily at the bag again.

Mickle knew he shouldn't give her any more because he wouldn't have any for the next five Sundays. But he

found his hand going inside the bag, and there it was, holding out another biscuit again!

Well, the girl ate five of those six biscuits, and Mickle was just handing her the very last one, when there came a shout from the gate, "Hi, Binny, hi! Where are you? Come along at once!"

The beggar-child jumped up. Her name was Binny, and it was her father who was calling her. She gave Mickle a quick hug and flew out into the garden. Her father was standing by the gate, waiting.

"This brownie-man has been so kind to me, Father!" cried the little girl. "Give him a reward. Please do!"

She bit her last biscuit and some crumbs fell to the ground beside the gate. The tramp trod them into the earth with his foot and muttered a few strange words. He looked at Mickle out of bright green eyes.

"Sometimes a bit of kindness grows and grows and brings us a reward we don't expect!" he said. "And sometimes it doesn't! But today there is magic in the wind, so maybe you'll be lucky!"

He nodded to Mickle and he and the beggar-child went dancing up the lane together, their rags blowing like dead leaves in the wind. Mickle shut the gate and went back to his warm kitchen. He was hungry – and all his biscuits were gone. Life was very sad.

He forgot all about the tramp and the beggar-child that spring. He never saw them again, and he worked so hard that he really hadn't time to think of anything except food and rest and work.

But one day he noticed a strong little shoot growing by his gate-post. He bent down to look at it. It was not like any seedling he had seen before. Perhaps it was a weed. Mickle thought he would pull it up. Then he thought he wouldn't. So he left it.

And to his enormous surprise it grew and grew very fast indeed, till in three weeks' time it was as high as the top of his gate! It sprouted into leaves. It grew higher still. It grew into a small tree, and Mickle had to walk under it when he went out of the gate. It was really most extraordinary!

He talked to his friends about it. They were used to magic, of course, but no one had ever seen a tree grow quite so quickly.

"It will flower soon and then we shall know what it is," said his friends. And the next week, sure enough, it did flower. It had funny flowers – bright red, with flat yellow middles.

The blossoms didn't last long. The red petals fell off, and the flat yellow middles grew larger. Everyone was most puzzled – till at last Dame Fanny gave a shout and slapped Mickle suddenly on the shoulder.

"It's a biscuit tree! That's what it is! A biscuit tree! Goodness me, one hasn't grown in the kingdom for about five hundred years! A biscuit tree, a biscuit tree!"

Well, Dame Fanny was right. It was a biscuit tree, and no mistake! The biscuits grew till they were ripe, and a sort of sugary powder came over them.

The Biscuit Tree

Then they were ready for picking.

And how Mickle enjoyed picking biscuits off his biscuit tree! You would have loved it too. He got some big and little tins from his grocer, lined them

167

with paper, and then picked the biscuits. He laid each one neatly in a tin, till the tin was full and he could put the lid on. Then he took up another tin and filled that. He did enjoy himself.

He gave a tin of biscuits to everyone in the village. This was just like kind old Mickle, of course. They were pat-a-cake biscuits, and for a long time nobody knew why the tree was a pat-a-cake biscuit tree, nor why it had grown at all. And then Pixie Lightfoot suddenly remembered that she had given Mickle some pat-a-cake biscuits some months back.

"What did you do with them?" she asked Mickle. "Did you eat them?"

"No," said Mickle. "I gave them all to a beggar-child."

"Did she drop any crumbs near your gate, where the biscuit tree is growing?" asked Lightfoot.

"Yes – she did – and I remember now, her father stamped them into the ground, and said that sometimes kindness grew its own reward – and he said that there was magic in the wind that day!" cried Mickle.

"Ah – now we know everything!" said Lightfoot. "It was your own bit of kindness that grew! From the biscuit-crumbs came your wonderful tree, Mickle. Oh, how marvellous! I do hope it goes on flowering year after year."

Well, it does, of course, so Mickle always has plenty of biscuits to eat, sell, or give away. Go by his gate in Misty Village during the summer and see his biscuits growing on the tree – he'll be sure to give you a pocketful if you wish him good morning!

169

Tippy's Trick

There was once a naughty elf called Tippy. He thought it was very funny to take things away from people and hide them. Then he would enjoy himself watching them hunting all over the place for what they had lost.

He took Dame Tinky's blue tablecloth off the line and pushed it down a worm-hole. Then he hid himself behind a daisy and watched the little old lady hunting everywhere for it.

He popped out at last and spoke to her. "What's the matter, Dame Tinky?"

"I'm looking for my blue tablecloth," said Dame Tinky. "It must have blown off the line. If you find it, Tippy, bring it back to me and I'll give you a penny."

Well, you can guess it didn't take Tippy long to find the tablecloth, because he had hidden it himself! He pulled it out of the worm-hole, and went to Dame Tinky's with it. She gave him a penny at once.

"This is fun," said bad Tippy. "I'll do a little more of this. Let me see, Mr Dumby usually stands his umbrella outside his door to dry when he has been out in the rain with it. I'll watch, and then I'll hide it away. Maybe he'll give me a penny, too, if I bring it back."

So he waited about, and when he saw Mr Dumby's little green umbrella standing in his front door porch to dry after he had taken it out in the rain, Tippy crept up very quickly and took

171

it. He stuffed it down the worm-hole again.

Well, Mr Dumby was upset to have lost his umbrella. He looked all about for it, and when he saw Tippy passing by, he called to him, "I've lost my umbrella. See if you can find it anywhere for me. I'll give you a penny if you do."

Well, Tippy rushed off to the worm-hole, pulled out the umbrella, and ran back with it. Mr Dumby gave him a penny, and was very pleased.

Then Tippy took a red shawl off the clothes-line in Mother Mickle's garden. He stuffed that down a worm-hole, too. Mother Mickle was very sad when she found that her best red shawl was gone.

She hunted everywhere. Tippy passed by and called out to her, "What are you looking for?"

"My best red shawl. It must have blown off the line although I pegged it there very firmly," said Mother Mickle sadly.

"What will you give me if I find it for you?" asked Tippy.

"A penny," said Mother Mickle.

"Say twopence," said Tippy. "It's a fine shawl, isn't it?"

"Well, twopence, then," said the old dame.

Tippy got his twopence, for it wasn't more than ten minutes before he was back with the shawl. Mother Mickle looked sadly at the shawl. It was very dirty. "I shall have to wash it again," she said.

Tippy thought it was a very easy way of earning money. He didn't think how naughty it was. He went on hiding things away and getting rewards of pennies when he brought them back. He had quite a lot of money to spend.

People began to say how strange it was that so many things vanished, and that Tippy always seemed to know where they were.

"I believe he takes them himself and hides them," said Jinky.

"Where does he hide them?" said Mother Mickle.

"We'll find out," said Jinky. But nobody could find out. When anything vanished they hunted everywhere, under the daisy-leaves, in the heart of the dandelion plants and everywhere – but they couldn't find the clever hiding-place that Tippy had chosen. A worm-hole was a very good place!

One night the Princess of Far-Away came to stay in the village where Tippy lived. The naughty little elf at once thought that if only he could hide something of hers he would get a very big reward for bringing it back. So he waited about outside the house where the pretty little princess was staying.

He saw a light go on in her bedroom. He waited till it went out again, and then he quietly climbed up a tree outside, and popped his hand in at the open window to see if he could feel anything on the table just inside.

"What luck," he thought to himself when he felt the princess's crown, and rings and necklaces, and bracelets! "I'll hide these, and then, when she says she will give a big reward, I'll bring them to her and say I found them."

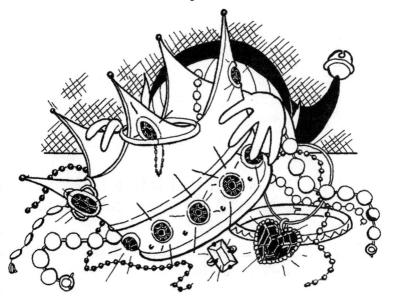

He slid down the tree with his treasures. He ran to his worm-hole and stuffed down all the things he had taken. He bent the grass over the hole, and went home to bed.

Well, it so happened that the princess woke up in the night and wanted a drink of water. She switched on her light – and, dear me, she saw that all her treasures had disappeared!

"My crown! My necklace! My rings!" she cried. "Robbers! Thieves!"

Soon the whole household was

176

awake. Mother Mickle, who lived next door, looked rather thoughtful. She had seen Tippy waiting about, and she just wondered if he had taken them to hide.

"I believe it's Tippy again," she said, and everyone agreed. But when they went to Tippy's house he was fast asleep in bed. So they all thought they would hunt about and find the missing treasures if they could.

They hunted all night – and meantime, a strange thing was happening. The day before, a spore from a toadstool nearby had blown into the worm-hole, and this spore began to grow. Now spores from toadstools or mushrooms are not really seeds, but they are able to grow into new toadstools or new mushrooms, just as seeds are able to grow into new plants.

And this new spore began to grow. It was to be a toadstool, and a big one too! It pushed itself up inside the worm-hole. It grew a nice little cap-like head. Its stalk grew long and pushed the head up. But there was something down that worm-hole that was in the way of the toadstool's growing.

That something was the treasure belonging to the Princess of Far-Away! The toadstool couldn't grow round the crown and the rings and all the rest – so it just pushed them upwards, as it grew.

No wonder the princess and her friends were astonished when they saw the toadstool growing up from the ground – for on the top of it were all the lost treasures! Toadstools grow in the night, very quickly – and this big toadstool grew in such a hurry that when daylight came, its head and stalk were far above the ground. Winking and blinking in the sun were the princess's rings and crown and necklaces and everything!

"Look at that!" said the princess. "All my lost things on that toadstool!"

Jinky looked at them. "They must have been hidden down a worm-hole," he said. "Very clever indeed. But the toadstool grew and pushed them up above the ground. Well, well – I'd very much like to know who took them and hid them!"

The princess put out her hand to take them, but Jinky stopped her.

"No," he said. "We'll just find out who hid them. Only one person besides ourselves knows who put the treasures down in that worm-hole – and that person is the thief. We'll do a bit of hiding ourselves now. We'll leave everything on the toadstool, and we'll all go and hide behind the daisies and dandelions. Then we'll see who comes

to find the treasures!"

So everyone hid carefully, and waited. They hadn't long to wait. Tippy woke up and dressed. He remembered the hidden treasures and set off to get them.

When he came to where his worm-hole was, he stared in amazement, for there was the toadstool, now very big indeed, spreading its cap to the sun, and carrying on its head everything that Tippy had pushed down the hole!

"Well, well!" said Tippy, aloud. "To think that a toadstool should grow up in the very hole where I hid everything. What a surprising thing! It's a good thing nobody came by and saw what had happened, or I wouldn't get that reward!"

"And you won't get it now!" shouted Jinky, popping up from behind a daisy. "You wicked elf! Now we know what you've been up to, now we know your hiding-place! If that toadstool hadn't grown up, we'd never have found you out!"

Tippy was marched off to prison. He was well punished, and he cried very bitterly. But nobody was sorry for him.

"You're a nasty, mean elf," they said. "You'd better turn over a new leaf, or you'll find yourself pushed out of Fairyland."

This was a dreadful threat, and Tippy did turn over a new leaf. He became a good and happy little elf – but there was always one thing he never liked – and that was a toadstool!

I wish I'd seen that toadstool growing up in the night, carrying its load of treasure!

Fly-Pie

There was once a big cat called Paddy. He was black-and-white, and had enormous whiskers. He was a great mouser – and, alas! He caught birds too.

But very soon the birds in the garden began to know Paddy, and to fly away as soon as he came near. The mice feared him, and ran to the fields. Even the rats wouldn't come into the garden. So Paddy couldn't catch anything at all.

He didn't really need to catch birds or mice, because his mistress fed him well. Three times a week she bought fish-scraps and boiled them for Paddy – and every day he had fresh milk, bacon rinds and scrapings of puddings, so he had plenty to eat.

But he loved catching birds and mice. One day he sat in the garden looking up into the blue sky – and up there, flying high, he saw hundreds of birds! Far more than he ever saw in the garden, thought Paddy.

He sat and watched them. They were swallows with curved wings and forked tails. You can see them any day in the summer and early autumn, if you look up into the sky.

"If only I could get those birds down here!" thought Paddy. "Tails and whiskers, what a fine feast I would have!"

He went to visit Kirry, the little pixie who lived under the hedge at the bottom of the garden.

"Kirry, what do those birds up in the sky eat?" he asked. "Do they nibble the clouds for their dinner – or eat a star or two?"

Kirry laughed loudly. "Those are swallows!" he said. "And they certainly don't eat the clouds or the stars – they catch flies all day long!"

"Oh, *flies*!" said Paddy, and he began to think. "Do they ever come down to earth, Kirry? There are such a lot of them up there."

"No – the swallows hardly ever come down to earth," said Kirry. "Only when they want mud for their nests, you know, and that's in the springtime."

"I wish I could get them down here," said Paddy. "I'd like to see them."

What he *really* meant was that he'd like to catch and eat them. But he didn't tell Kirry that, because Kirry loved the birds.

"Well – you won't get the swallows down here unless you give them as many flies as they can catch up there!" said Kirry.

"Oh," said Paddy, and he began to think hard. "Kirry," he said, "if I catch you a lot of flies, will you make me a fly-pie please? And send a message to the swallows to ask them to come down to tea here and eat the fly-pie?"

"Well, that's very kind of you, Paddy," said Kirry, pleased. "Yes – I'll certainly make a fly-pie for you."

So for the next few days Paddy caught flies instead of mice or birds! There were a great many of the noisy bluebottles about just then, and many Daddy-long-legs, which the grown-ups hated because their grubs ate the roots

185

of plants. So Paddy had a fine time catching these flies, and soon Kirry had enough to make a big fly-pie for the swallows.

He sent a message to the birds. "Please come down to tea tomorrow. There is a big fly-pie for you!"

The swallows twittered in the greatest excitement "Fly-pie! Fly-pie! Did you hear that? We'll go and eat it, eat it, eat it! We'll go and eat it, eat it, eat it!"

So they sent a message back to Kirry. "Yes! We'll all come down to-morrow to eat your nice fly-pie. Thank you very much!"

Kirry told Paddy. Paddy sharpened his claws and licked his lips. He would wait under the hedge for the swallows – and then spring out when they came, and catch dozens and dozens of them! What a feast he would have! He looked at the fly-pie which Kirry had baked. It looked fine, with a big crust on top, and a little pattern round the edge of the crust.

"They'll be here at four o'clock tomorrow," said Kirry. "Put a new bow of ribbon on, Paddy, and wash yourself well. It will be quite a party. It's so kind of you to think of fly-pie for the swallows!"

Paddy grinned to himself. Yes, he had thought of a meal of fly-pie for the swallows – but he had also thought of a meal of swallows for himself!

The next afternoon Paddy was well-hidden under the hedge. Kirry put out the fly-pie, and put ready a little knife to cut it with. Now everything was ready. Only the guests had to come.

But they didn't come! No – not a swallow came! Kirry waited and waited – and Paddy hid and waited too. But no swallow flew down to the fly-pie! Kirry looked up into the sky. It was quite empty of birds! Not a swallow darted in the air up there. It was very, very strange.

"Paddy!" called Kirry. "It's funny – but all the swallows have gone. I can't see a single one!"

Paddy came out, swinging his tail angrily. "*Gone*!" he said. "What do you mean, 'gone'? Just when I was looking forward to a good meal, too!"

"A good meal?" said Kirry,

astonished. "What *do* you mean? A good meal of what? I thought the fly-pie was for the swallows!"

"A good meal of swallows, silly!" squealed Paddy, in a temper. "Are you so foolish that you didn't know that the fly-pie was only a trap to catch swallows for me?"

"Oh! You wicked cat!" cried Kirry. "No – I didn't know that at all, or I would never have made the fly-pie for you! Now see what you have done! The swallows must have heard of your wicked trap – and they have all gone! Not one is left! Maybe they will never, never come back."

Paddy felt rather scared. Certainly the swallows had gone, there was no doubt about that – and how dreadful it would be if people got to know that he, Paddy, had driven them away because of his trap!

Paddy began to slink away, ashamed of his trick. But Kirry was very angry and shouted after him, "You're a bad cat! I don't want you for a friend any more! You and your fly-pie! Here, take it – you're the only one likely to have it now!"

He threw the fly-pie after Paddy. It broke over his head – and Paddy had to spend a most unpleasant half-hour licking the fly-pie off his thick black-and-white fur. Well, it served him right!

As for the swallows, they hadn't heard about the trap at all! You see, a cold wind had begun to blow the night before, and the chief of the swallows had decided that it was time to leave our country and fly to warmer countries far away!

So, with many twitterings, the swallows had gathered together, and then, with one accord, they had risen into the air and flown to the south! They would come back again in the spring – but Paddy didn't know that!

He just sat licking the unpleasant fly-pie off his fur, thinking, "Well, never again will I try a trick like this! No, never again."